IN HIS OWN WORDS

Shaun Ryder

SHAUN RYDER... IN HIS OWN WORDS

Exclusive distributors:

Book Sales Limited
0-9 Frith Street, London W1V 5TZ, UK

Music Sales Corporation
257 Park Avenue South, New York, NY 10010, USA

Music Sales Pty Limited
120 Rothschild Avenue, Rosebery, NSW 2018, Australia

Exclusive distributors to the music trade only:

Music Sales Limited
8-9 Frith Street, London W1V 5TZ, UK

ISBN 0.7119.6815.2
Order No. OP48055

Compilation and introduction by Mick Middles
Edited by Chris Charlesworth, Omnibus Press

Designed by Pearce Marchbank, Studio Twenty
Computer layout by Ben May, Studio Twenty

Picture research by Nikki Russell, Omnibus Press

All photographs by London Features International
except pages 2, 3, 7, 19, 28-29, 87, 88, 90-91,
92, 96 and front cover by SIN

Printed in Great Britain by
Page Bros Ltd, Norwich, Norfolk

Visit Omnibus Press at
http://www.musicsales.co.uk

OMNIBUS PRESS

SHAUN RYDER... IN HIS OWN WORDS

There was not a hint, not a flicker, of a bright future on Shaun Ryder's horizon when, at the age of fifteen, he fell from his Swinton school into the deadening cul-de-sac of a messenger boy's job with the Post Office. By this time, and by his own admission on these pages, he thought of little more than instant gratification... of drugs and money... of clothes and music.

A criminal lifestyle seemed to offer the only way out of the surrounding drudgery.

Shaun Ryder knew from that early age, and perhaps even sooner, that he simply wouldn't be able to cope with an ordinary life and, as the intelligence which would begin to shine from him in later years simply wasn't picked up by the educational system, all seemed hopeless.

Perhaps the clue lay with his father. Derek, himself a loveable rogue, forever dreamt of stardom, and performed as a bass player in various Merseybeat combos. Later, when 'having a go' as a stand up comic, Ryder Senior was famously beaten in a talent contest by a precocious young lass named Lisa Stansfield. Derek's shadow would hang heavily over the career of his offspring... as a muse perhaps, or as a springboard. Shaun Ryder inherited his father's sense of eternal hope but he was simultaneously fired by a determination not to make the same mistakes.

The odds against his first band, Happy Mondays, actually 'making

it' were simply staggering. Falling together in Little Hulton as the Eighties unfolded, they were little more than a torrid mess of street culture camaraderie.

A gang, in every sense of the word, they instantly achieved uniqueness by being, surely, the only band in rock history who formed as a basis from which they could practice drug peddling and various related activities.

They couldn't have known it at the time, but this gang mentality, coupled with their inability to produce the wonderful sounds that were soundtracking their lives – a disparate blend of Funkedelic, Captain Beefheart, Sex Pistols, Joy Division, James Brown etc – would provide their unique appeal. The early Happy Mondays recordings are fuelled more by sheer frustration than anger. But they were fascinating for another reason. On the top of that shambolic sound – indeed, very much at an excruciating forefront on their debut album, perversely produced by John Cale – lay a virtually tuneless voice spouting all manner of weird, wonderful, meaningless in-jokery. The voice and the words of Shaun Ryder. Immediately we could tell that there was nothing else quite like it on Earth. Simply by providing the band with the title of that first album – Squirrel And G-Man Plastic Face Carn't Smile (White Out), complete with mis-spelling – Ryder had proved that he could create something abstractly appealing from the mess of local culture which surrounded him.

As the Happy Mondays' story, a gloriously messy tale of unbridled hedonism, brilliance and sheer cheek, unfolded, the personality of Shaun Ryder came more and more to the fore.

Despite his heroin addiction, despite a number of other addictions too, or perhaps even because of them, we began to glimpse a curious wisdom emerging from Ryder's inarticulate music press ramblings. Paradoxically, Shaun Ryder, a man with a growing reputation for his seemingly unstoppable capacity to imbibe, also seemed to display a consider-able measure of common sense.

For a while this really did seem very odd indeed. We had him, or so we thought, pinned down as a loveable miscreant. An oddity who had struck it lucky. We never, in our wildest dreams, thought that it would last.

Surely his fuse would swiftly burn to a frazzled ember, leaving Happy Mondays as little more than an entertaining memory, a rock/dance delicacy perhaps, a fading reminder of teenage days in floppy denim.

When the band spectacularly imploded, the rumours about Shaun Ryder bounced about Manchester and the rock world, like a pinball. He was a fat, washed-out, broke smack addict, who had simply blown his chance. The rumours were understandable, but they didn't take into account the sheer resilience of the man in question. While other former Mondays members ranted in the music press about what they were going to do next – which wasn't much, as it turned out – Shaun Ryder quietly set about assembling his second career, as front man of the juiciest, daftest, funkiest, most absurd pop/rock/dance act of the Nineties, the mighty, unparalleled state of party known to the world as Black Grape.

Whereas Happy Mondays had started to crumble the moment they started to take themselves seriously, Black Grape adopted a refreshingly loose and friendly approach. And in the music press, Ryder would re-emerge as a more than accomplished interviewee,

a wise old wicked owl whose capacity to deliver a rich seam of wordy outbursts was matched only by his fellow Salfordian, Mark E Smith.

The quotes presented here, many of them contradictory and, perhaps rather unfairly plucked from the context of a hundred nights of inebriated ramblings, see Shaun Ryder emerge from the depths of hedonism before finally beginning to look like a true winner. Many of them are hilarious and not, I'd suggest, to be taken too seriously. For Ryder's tongue was always jammed in his cheek, not least during his famous outburst in the NME, when his gritty Salfordian banter was seized upon by a gruesome politically correct readership who wrongly condemned him as homophobic. In his later (Black Grape) quotes, Ryder emerges as an unlikely family man, quite clearly enjoying an idyllic country life in Ireland although, one senses, if only now and then, a wedge of hedonistic desire creeping into his sentences.

As he edges towards forty, Shaun Ryder seems both content and restless, dabbling here and there in film acting, in the cult of celebrity and as Black Grape front man.

Clearly he doesn't know what awaits him past that forty year threshold. But equally, at no point in his thirteen years of stardom, or in his entire life one presumes, has he seemed more in control.
Mick Middles

The Little Brats Of Little Hulton

I remember the time when Amanda Gibbons and her friends were having a dolls' tea party for 'er seventh birthday. Dead prim and soft, fairy cakes an' all that shit. So we... me and Bez it were, climbed over the fence with our Action Men and threw mud all over them 'till they all ran away, screaming, crying... mind you, that were some time ago. **1996**

I used to see Gaz and Paul Davis knocking about when I was a kid. I remember seeing Paul D when he was about six years old. I was riding along the road on me bike and I saw this kid with a dead little body and a dead massive head. That was Paul. Bez is from around the area as well. He used to go to Wardley High School along with Gaz, Paul D and Mark. Me and our kid went to Ambrose, which is ten minutes down the road from Wardley. **1993**

I left school before I was fifteen. I got a job as a messenger boy for the Post Office, did that for a few years, then after that, nothing. We used to deliver telegrams around the area which was OK. When you get to eighteen you have to become a proper postman working mad hours, like, for £100 and that's fucking garbage. So I didn't do anything after that. **1996**

Bez's dad. A right cunt he was. A CID inspector. Bez would have to sneak into the dole because if his dad saw him, he'd come out of the house and fuckin' beat him up. Hammer him. The guy is an evil Scouse fucking pig. **1986**

Being a postal messenger was a laugh. We used to deliver telegrams and generally fuck around. But I would see these guys, year in, year out, trudging through Swinton, bags piled high. They were good guys, I liked them but I thought their lives were becoming increasingly sad, year after year. I know that was expected of me, in a way but I had enough of me dad in me to know that I wanted something better. I wasn't sure what, but I wasn't going down that road, no way. **1987**

The last car I stole was a Ford Granada, a monster car. It was brand new, on the East Lancs Road. I slipped behind the wheel and hurtled off down the road. Immediately a police car began chasing us so, in a panic, I swung it into a cul-de-sac before going straight through a wall and a privet hedge. I staggered out of the car, onto a lawn where an elderly couple were standing. Trust me. His son happened to be a policeman. **1988**

I once saw a UFO. In Little Hulton it was. We was walking to school, hoping to catch the 7 am bus and we looked up and saw this thing that went "Per-chung, per-chung! Pwa! Pow!" It was a glowing thing and we were watching it and it was looking at us. Then, Chunn! It was gone. I've seen a few things but people always say, "You're on drugs" when you see a UFO in a tennis court in Didsbury. But I know what I've seen. And they watch you, they do keep a check on you. I reckon we made contact with them in the Sixties. You see! Even you think I'm nuts for saying that. Only a few of us know the truth. **1996**

We used to go ratting. Our house was behind the sewage farm. We used to shoot 'em with air pistols. Great fun. Ever looked behind a sewage farm? It stinks. You gotta have somewhere to play. You do these things when you are 12 or 13. You see all these rats running about. So the only thing to do is to start shooting them. Rats. It's OK to kill them... Cats... Cats are different. Kids who go round spearing cats are just dickheads. Cats are top. Cats talk and everything. They can talk to you. I've just read a book. In the book, right, it tells you what they mean.

Like, they go 'Meeeoooowwww' and that means 'Let me out, I've had me food.'

Look mate, I'm not gonna knock you. I might come round to your house and you'll have all these rats running round. You'll show me how to talk to them. I'm not gonna call you a dickhead. If you can prove to me those rats are all right, I'll get into it. But I don't like rats, I don't mind sayin'. There's a difference, you see, between white rats and 'orrible, squirmy, scumbag, gyppo rats that run about in fields and live in sewage farms. You don't have to feel sorry for rats. They can eat your brains out. You don't have to feel sorry for something that can do that to you. **1989**

We used to do some stupid things when we was growing up, which I now regret. I blew up mice by attaching them to gas pipes. Killed the science teacher's animals. But you learn. Kids from 13 to 19 are walking time bombs where I come from, a council estate in Swinton. Psychotic bastards. I'd lock them up. We've all been in the nick for this and that, so what? Where I come from it's just part of living. **1989**

I wouldn't say I was always on the nick... I learned how to deal with money and goods and things. I remember when I got my job as a post boy I was 15. My first week's wages was £17. When I was 14 years old, I was having £500 to £600 a week away. The reason I got the job was because I'd done a TDA – which is take and driving away – and smashed the car into a wall of somebody's house, and so getting a job as a messenger boy kept me from getting nicked. And to get a fucking £17 wage after the money I'd been used to was a big kick in the balls for me. **1989**

What would I have done if music hadn't rescued me? I don't know. It just depends on how clever you are, dunnit? Whether you get caught or don't get caught. I'm not saying I would have been Mister fucking robbing banks or any of that bollocks, but, one, I have certainly not got a qualification and, two, the jobs that I'd have to do wouldn't satisfy my lust for money. When I was a 13 or 14 year old lad, I was the richest kid in my class at school. **1996**

I loved *That'll Be The Day* and *Stardust*. Yeah, man. I spent me days wagging off school, watching them films. Put it this way. At the time I was going watching films on money I'd stolen and I'd be sitting there, eating hamburgers, thinking, fuck me, that's a good life. Especially

when it gets to Stardust and it gets to being the rock 'n' roll thing. I thought, that's fucking great, that. I wasn't put off when he (David Essex) ODs at the end. He was a pop star when he got into drugs. I was already doing drugs. **1996**

A friend of ours had gone in the army when they used to do the German stretch in the Seventies and he'd come out and hung around in Hamburg and Holland and he started getting into the porno thing. The magazines and the films. I was a fourteen-year-old lad who thought, I'd fuck off to Amsterdam and do some porn. I wasn't going to any college or anything like that. **1987**

I lost me virginity with me socks on... and Docs on. Cos, don't forget, in them days the pants were really wide, your parallels and all that. Eight hole Docs on and no way were my eight hole Docs coming off in some underground car park. Just the pants off, man, with the Docs on. I thought it was great. **1996**

Me and this lad were walking around Manchester one day with boxes of them rat poison pellets, and we hated fucking pigeons being all over the place. I'm not so bad now, but when I was younger they used to put me off me food, man. So we went around feeding them all with bread stuffed with poison. Then, the next day it's in the *Daily Mirror*. 'Sick maniacs poison pigeons.' They were dropping out of the skies.

A few years before that, when we were eleven, we torched this school building, this new science lab that had cost so much to build. The day after it had been officially opened and everything, we torched it, burnt it down. That was in the paper as well. I was only about fucking ten. But, listen, if there's any comebacks about this, Liam and Noel said they burgled houses, like. 'Shaun Ryder, we are going to press charges against you torching down the school.' I'd say, I made it up 'cos I'm a pop star and we've got to make stories up. **1990**

Me and Bez used to live together. It wasn't like The Monkees though. The Monkees had fucking windows in their house, we had fuck all. It was terrible. Salford and Eccles, we had a couple of flats that were just fucking horrible. I don't find anything glamourous about that at all. I don't look back at it with nostalgia. Some days, or weeks when we didn't get any money and the only buzz you could get was a 70p tube of gas. **1990**

24-Hour Party People

I used to be called 'Horse' at school then the name got put onto our kid and our dad became Horseman. Then I became known as 'X' when I was 19. It was like a piss take. People used to shout out at me "SHAUN" when I was selling draw and things. So people started shouting 'X' at me to try to make me paranoid. 'Knobhead' stuck for Paul D, actually he's known as 'Peni' now. Cow has got a few names like 'Moose' and 'Bastard' and 'Daisy'. Gaz is just 'Ronny' because his last name is Whelan. **1987**

The band began when I was nineteen. I know Gaz and Knobhead (Paul Davis) were still at school. We didn't go through line up changes, really. I do remember Paul D coming up to me in the street and saying, "Is Gaz Whelan in your band?" I went, "Yeah, do you know him?" And Paul D said, "Yeah, he's my best mate but he's shit. He shouldn't be in your band. What does he do? Play drums? I can do it better than him. I wanna be in it." **1992**

We used to practice in this old school. I told Gaz that his mate, Paul D, had been mithering me and that he was well weird. Anyway, Paul D turned up, didn't he? So we told him he had to play keyboards. He got a small keyboard but he couldn't do anything with it. Next week, Paul D came and told us that he'd got a bass and that he wanted to play that. I told him "Our kid's got a bass and he can play it already, you can't, you dickhead, so fuck off." Anyway, Paul D eventually settled down on keyboards. **1992**

The first gig I went to... I think it was Be-Bop Deluxe sometime around '73 or '75, Manchester Free Trade Hall. It was alright. It was just a thrill just getting a ticket and actually going there. **1997**

The worst record I ever made was 'This Feeling' or 'Delightful'. They are terrible and cheesy. They are the first things the Mondays ever did. I know we were doing speed but, fucking hell, they are about three thousand miles per hour. Blame it on the whizz. **1997**

The first single we did was 'Delightful' in '85. Between forming the band and that nothing really happened. It was just us having a good time. All we did the band for was to get pissed, have a jam. We didn't even want to play gigs... there was nobody at our first gig (at The Gallery, Manchester), and it was so crap that I felt a bit embarrassed. I never felt we'd really ever get anywhere... I wasn't even sure it was a band. Well, it wasn't a fucking band, was it? It shouldn't have happened really, should it? But it did... somehow.

Maybe, in not really being bothered, we came across as quite honest in an unusual way. It was more natural. I think our second gig was a Battle Of The Bands night at The Hacienda. Tony Wilson saw we were nervous and said, 'Don't worry about it, you've won already'. He wanted us for Factory. I kept wondering why! Why would Factory want us? I thought they were fucking stupid. **1990**

That actual song, 'Delightful', was slow, spacey. I'd guess you'd call it disorientating, like our music is now. Mike Pickering was the producer. We had never seen the inside of a studio before. We all did loads of whizz and the whole thing just speeded up and it didn't come out right. Mike got a good sound but it wasn't us. And that's when we realised that, when you record things get taken out of your hands a bit. Not Mike's fault, don't get me wrong, but even though we didn't have a fucking clue about studios, or playing instruments, or vocals or anything like that... we still knew what we wanted to sound like.

From then on we knew we would have to be more forceful. True it helps if you can play your fucking instruments but that wasn't important. We were getting better in that respect. We suddenly realised that we were the customers in a studio situation. No way should you find

that intimidating... 'cos you are fucking paying for it. Yes... I learnt that pretty fucking fast. **1990**

The first proper gigs we did were with New Order. But we were not trailing around in the shadow of them because when we go out with them, we get fucking food, booze and treated right. They were the only pop stars we knew. We thought everyone in the business was like that. **1990**

We didn't know how a band worked at first. We didn't even know how a band rehearsed properly, so I once went along to see The Colourfield in rehearsal in Liverpool, just to see how it was done. I learned a lot from Terry. People thought he didn't care how he looked in front of an audience but that wasn't the case. He worked a crowd really well. **1987**

We would hang around with Terry Hall in about 1985. It was good to go out with him and see how professional he was and learn a bit. Up until then we had done a couple of gigs with New Order but we didn't actually know how proper bands of musicians worked because most of our gigs were one-offs. So going around with Colourfield, watching Terry and how he was and how he controlled audiences was how we got our first real insight. Also Fun Boy Three had been one of our favourite bands when we were younger. So it was a boost for us and Terry was dead cool. **1996**

We used to listen to Echo And The Bunnymen and Joy Division and New Order. We were also into Orange Juice still and dance music and funk music. Northern soul, The Beatles and Stones. All that stuff we still listen to now. I guess pop music in general and dance because even then we would spend a lot of time going to dance clubs. Pips in Manchester in the Seventies had nine different rooms in it from a punk room to a Roxy and Bowie room to a disco room and northern soul. So you had nine different sorts of music going on and some of that

music had sunk into us. The place is now called The Konspiracy. **1990**

When we first found out that we were going from one place to another in a van and getting beer money and petrol money paid and staying out for the night in a hotel, that was great. We didn't see it as art or money or whatever. We'd all go around fucking Germany and everywhere on a bus for fucking £200.
    At that point, it was a cover. We used to steal all the leather jackets and shoes and things like that. Our wages were whatever we got. Especially when we went over to Switzerland, you didn't have to start doing any daft thieving or any credit cards or anything. You could just walk into a restaurant, pick some mother-fucker's coat up that they've just hung on the door. It would be a £700 coat and, inside their wallet would be there. That was really us. That was how we got paid.
    It is true, as well, that when we started off, me dad did rob all our equipment. He used to go into social clubs with a screw driver and unplug all the fucking speakers and things and then walk off with the best amp. **1992**

There's Manchester and there's South Manchester. Moss Side is more conge-nial than Little Arndale 'cos you've got clubs open for twenty-four hours. It's hard to adjust, at times, to visiting that central side of town, especially as you hate thinking, hate worrying and hate it all. **1986**

HALLELUJAH! SHAUN AND BEZ, 1989

Squirrel & G-Man 24-Hour Party People Plastic Face Carn't Smile (White Out)

Squirrel is the name of Knobhead's mum because she looks like a squirrel. G-man is Bez's dad, 'cos he's a cop. Twenty-Four Hour Party People is what we used to call ourselves even before the band. It was like a title for whizz freaks. 'Plastic Face' and 'Carn't Smile' is just like a mad sayin' all sunk into one. Didn't know it was spelt wrong at first. I thought of the album title and all the rest were going, 'No way, you're off your head.' They like it now and I liked it then because it just sounded mental. **1989**

Tony (Wilson) brought John Cale in to produce us. He was all right, a nice bloke. Bez and I knew about John Cale. The rest knew of The Velvets but didn't know who John Cale was. I guess Tony picked Cale because of the drug connection. **1989**

'Tart Tart' is the name of a bird that died who adopted me and Bez. Her name was Dinah. She used to look after me and Bez when we had nowhere to live. She used to deal drugs but she ended up dying of a brain haemorrhage. She really used to like the band. **1987**

We never write songs as such. Lyrics just come out of me head. Most of them are just words strung together like. They just fit. Just childish rhymes. Like this mate of mine who used to go in the chippy and ask for "Rabbit dropping pooh pooh pooh cacky plop" for his dinner. This woman would have to guess what he wanted. That's our brain. That's how it has always been.

There's a lot of words in our songs that have got fuck all to do with the songs. Ever listened to Abba? Abba couldn't speak English when they wrote those songs, could they? Like me, I couldn't really write a song that was about some-thing. I'm not that clever. I'm a rapper, whatever. I admire people with a few brains, though. I wish I had brains, could have been a brain surgeon.

Most of the songs are like short stories from *The Twilight Zone*. They are not about anything real. Little black comedies. I'm quite happy singing something that's meaningless as long as it's witty. You put your own pictures to it. **1990**

The fact is though, we all began to get this big reputation as being a daft bunch of cunts around town after that first album, as if it was all part of an act. But it wasn't a fuckin' act at all, man. It was no different from what we was doing before, but suddenly people started to recognise us. And that was a right fuckin' pain in the arse because we still had no money. We was going out, selling draw and being in a band wasn't helping us at all.

I never knew it would be like that. To be in the *NME* and *Sounds* all the time. I thought that meant that loads of money would come in. But it meant absolutely fuck all. So we had to survive, man. Then there were a couple of times when, getting bigger, you know, making it really did seem to sneak through. S'pose underneath it all we enjoyed being recognised. We wanted fame, course we fucking did. **1992**

House was already happening, even when we did 'Squirrel and G-Man'. We were all copping off to 'Nude Nights' at The Hacienda and obviously it was sinking in. It's like, when we were playing or recording we'd have ideas in our heads but we couldn't get them all out into our instruments. It's like you can see something but when you come to try and draw it on a piece of paper you can't. So that was the same with our music. We

knew what we wanted it to feel like but we were just learning on the early stuff how to put it together.

I haven't listened to 'Squirrel and G-Man' for years. All I can remember is that there are a lot of spaces. We were trying to get a Doors type of groove but make it dance music as well. The stuff may sound like indie rock now but at the time indie rock was more a tighter faster winkle pickered finger and we were putting out spacious things. So we were still on the same trip as we are now. **1992**

The Manchester scene? There's them and there's fucking us. I'm not saying that we are any better but, like a lot of bands seem to be in some kind of muso's fucking club. We aren't anything like that. We hang around with our mates, we are just like them and they are all we'll ever need. I'm not saying we aren't flash gits and we want to get on. But that's the point.

I'll tell you what, we can't be smug 'cos we ain't got a fuckin' penny between us and some of the lads who have started to follow us are dressed in this dead smart gear and that. I'm always thinking, "Fuck me, I wish I could afford that". So we sell 'em some stuff, you know, going into clubs with loads of stuff in little packets. We are just drug dealers who happen to be in a band rather than the other way around. None of the other bands can fucking say that, can they? But if we ever do make it, like New Order, there will still be us and this gang around us. I know everyone says that but that's how it is with us and always will be. **1986**

'Kuff Dam'... the title came from picking up some porno book years ago and there was 'Mad Fuck. Film Story.' So we spelt it backwards. **1987**

We are all obsessed with sex. It's to do with dirty women down Little Arndale. Thirty-five-year-old divorcees with two kids who give you warts. In fact I've still got a very big one to prove it. **1987**

Bummed

Eighty-six was an important time. I fucked off to Amsterdam for a year and grew me hair. I had me first E in the Dam. It was one of them real tiny, dead good Doves. I felt really great. Dead happy and I had this thing of being clean, all shaved and that lot. Got rid of the fucking goatee. And I didn't want to drink beer. I had Perrier water and didn't really feel anything. All I knew was that I felt fantastic. Then I kind of learnt the buzz. **1996**

E changed our lives financially. We had a couple of years when we had really struggled for dough. Petty pilfering, small time drug dealing, all that lot. Me and Bez would go to them pubs where all the dancing-round-the-handbag chicks was. I'd sit at a table and me an' Bez'd keep 'em talking and I'd have a pair of moccasins with no socks on, right? I'd take me shoe off and open the chick's bag with me toes, get the purse out, have the money and it'd be, 'see ya girls'. Sometimes you'd feel a bit sorry for them and they'd have, say, £60 – I tell you man, girls always have money – so I'd take £40 and put £20 back so at least they'd have their cab fare home. **1996**

I'd dabbled about the heroin since I was a sixteen-year old kid. I took it with me mate at first. He threw up. I didn't. But, back then, I was limited by the amount of money I had. Sometimes I'd get a £5 or £10 wrap but I didn't always have the dough so that sort of naturally looked after itself. I'd have days off. But once we started getting popular with the band, me mates used to give it to me to sample so there would be plenty of it about. **1992**

We only put those things (drug references) into our songs, not because we want to write about them but because, sometimes, we don't have any other ideas. Most of the nicknames we've got in our songs are made up by Gaz or Knobhead. The thing is we all like it. We didn't want to be completely corny. It just didn't turn

out like that. It's the same with 'Lazyitis'. We wanted it to be a really corny pop song, a toy one. Again it didn't turn out that way but got kind of fucked. The version with Karl Denver is a lot closer to the idea we had in mind in the first place. **1992**

That's what we call country and western. Some cunt from Preston. It's rhyming slang, you dickhead. If you write a country and western tune, you've gotta write double shit corny words. So that's what I did. It's a corny story innit? Just like any corny country and western song. She fell in love with me and I ran away. Haha. **1988**

We was caned on E when we were making *'Bummed'*. And I must stress here it wasn't the right thing to do. We didn't really know what it was and it wouldn't be right to do it with Es now. But then you'd have one in the morning, one at twelve o'clock, one at five, one early night time and one later on.

Nobody had E in Manchester before we brought it back. There was about ten of us and we'd all be stood in the corner of The Hac (ienda) buzzin' away. Trying to sell something at £25 a time is madness. But that's what they went for. They was costing us a couple of pence each but they went for £25. But no one wants to buy something they've never heard of for £25. So what we did was sort out all our mates – we gave hundreds away – and we was eating them like mad. Then over the next month, fuck me, they'd come skipping in and queue up for them. And by then the Hac was fucking packed. **1989**

It's brilliant the way all those music barriers have been kicked in. I reckon it's down to drugs. E particularly. They are now accepting 'Wrote For Luck' in the south. To be honest... I didn't know much about the remixes of that. Vince (Clarke) wanted to do a remix of that and 'Twenty-four Hour Party People' so we just said, 'sure'. It was good but a bit poppy for us. I really like the Paul Oakenfold mix though. It's the kind of thing I'd like to dance to. I think that people up north should listen a bit more to what's happening to clubs in London. Seems to me that the DJs in London – the Balearic ones – are mixing up all sorts of different music. Which is proper. Makes life exciting. **1989**

I do know that when *'Bummed'* came out, two years ago, I had already knocked down my consumption of E. When we did *'Bummed'* I could still eat three Es a day but we were a lot calmer than before. **1990**

'Bummed'. It's fuller man. We were more in command of what we were doing. With or without Martin (Hannett). The first album was more about playing with things. Messin' about, trying stuff out. If it was up to me I wouldn't have made anything before 'Tart Tart'. I wouldn't have done that first album. That seems now like... I dunno, something out of childhood. Like looking at an old school essay that you are now really embarrassed by... no... no... it's not that bad. But I will never be able to listen to the fucking thing again, though. People say it was a really important album and all that stuff. Well, maybe it did kind of capture a scene... but that doesn't stop it from being shite, does it? **1988**

'Bummed' was just a stupid, silly little stupid name. We wanted it to be offensive and we thought loads of people would take it the wrong way. We was quite shocked when nobody really took any notice. Well, nobody apart from the odd feminist hackette but no one gives a shit what they think. **1990**

He's a fookin' mate to the Mondays, Martin (Hannett). He's great when he's with us, man. Mind, he likes workin' with us 'cos we give him a lot of E during sessions, right? E sorts him right out. During the 'Hallelujah' sessions we were

givin' him two a day and this were when they were twenty-five quid a go, right? But it were worth it 'cos he kept sayin' "I can't feel anything but I'm in a fuckin' great frame of mind". Plus it stopped him getting too bladdered. **1989**

Tony's (Wilson, Factory boss) just a businessman, really. Someone like him... I mean, he likes us. At least I think he does. But he's got to use the drugs angle to sell us. I mean, what the fook could Gaz, Bez or me be without someone like Tony exploiting us? We wouldn't 'ave jobs, 'cos we can't do fookin' jobs. That's just a fookin' fact, right? I mean, he's exploiting us right, but we're exploiting the situation he's given to us 'cos like two years ago we 'ad to 'ave drugs on our person 'cos we were sellin' 'em, right? So if you got caught it were a bigger problem. 'Cos it were bigger amounts we were carrying'.

But like now we always carry the name of a good solicitor around with us. I've got this card, right, an' I just show it the filth when they come prying. Whereas before when they'd search me they'd always find, like, forty-seven plastic bags and no solicitors card... foookin' hassles, y'knowharrraaaamean? **1990**

HAPPY MONDAYS

Pills Thrills 'n' Bellyaches...
Big Time Mondays

The chicks are always attracted to me enormous charisma. **1990**

Have been on tour for thirteen month... am really fuckin' knackered. **1990**

(To early *MM* journalist) Are we meant to say thank you for you coming round here? 'Cos we fucking well won't. That's the way it's got to be 'cos we aint gonna be bending down on one knee. Lot of bands do that. You can see it in their interviews, drives me fucking mental. You should be thanking us, mate. **1988**

Our real friends were not in the least bit bothered about us going on *Top Of The Pops*. In fact they were fucking well made up. It was all those fucking trendy types, the floppy fucking students. They were the ones saying, 'Oh I don't like them anymore, they have gone on Top Of The Pops.' Fucking cunts. All of them. They were never real fans. It's like, over in England, when someone gets a nice car and some bastard smashes it up because they haven't got one. Shit pots. It's just daft. They've never had a real life, them idiots. I never wanted them near the band in the first place, jumped up tossers living in a dream world.

This is real for us. It's our only way out, isn't it? I'm sorry for people who are still stuck in the shit but I can hardly take the whole of working class Salford with me, can I? They should cherish the success. That's what it has always been about. Not some trendy, studenty, hippie idea that we shouldn't sell out. Fuck. I thought we were past all that. The whole point of it is to sell out or else fuck off and let someone else have a bash. **1990**

You'll find no rivalry here, between us and The Roses. Well the only rivalry is, like, over clothes, really. There's always been a bit of a race on to see who's got the best, flashiest clothes, right, and what part of the world these clothes come from. 'Cos we are both flash cunts, y'knowwarrramean? **1990**

We've chosen to live like this and that's it. We're just playing a game, the same game we've been playing for a long time. That's the trouble with being on *Top Of The Pops*, though. Someone in the force might get clever. The police are thick. They are dirt thick. We all know that and Bez's dad's a nasty fuckin' high rankin' CID officer. A real nasty bastard. One of those fookin' workin' class cunts as likes to dish it out. Now this bastard hasn't seen Bez for five or six years. He doesn't know anything about him or Happy Mondays. Until he sees us on *Top Of The Pops*... **1990**

We just see the Mondays as a licence to do what we want, right now as much as possible. The police and that can't do worse to us than what they've already done, like. And if I do get banged up, it's not like it's something that's never happened before. Jail's nothing new to me, man. Bird, like, it's all down to how you use your time really. I mean you can read a few books. Or study a foreign language. It's a bit of a lark, really. **1990**

The Mondays, we've been friends for over ten years, pal. There's no one else we'd rather be with for doing the things we wanna do. When you have been friends for that long... well, for a start you can take the piss out of each other somethin' rotten and get away with it. Gaz can call me some right snide things and I won't fuckin' crack him one. **1990**

But like our keyboard player's off his fookin' trolley. Daft as a fookin' brush. He's a top lad, our Paul, but 'e don't 'alf talk some fookin' toss sometimes. You 'ave to tell 'im "Shoot the fook up." If 'e were 'ere now 'e'd be over 'ere talkin'

daft. And you'd probably hate him 'cos 'e's a bit of a bastard too. You just 'ave to say "Shurrup our Paul and listen to what yer sayin', ya great fookin' knobhead." But 'e's daft. That's just 'is way. **1990**

People keep asking us about Manchester... we have never ever really stayed in Manchester. We get around, pal. London... Paris. Bez was found living in the fookin' Sahara Desert in a fookin' cave, man. It's the fookin' truth, that. Manchester's just where we are from. **1990**

Our sound's all sorts, really. Funkadelic, 'One Nation Under A Groove' being eaten by a giant sandwich... that were fookin' tops, that... northern soul... punk rock... Jimi Hendrix... fookin' Captain Beefheart. An' lots of drugs on top o' that. It was through Bez with E... just. Get them down yer neck son, go on, more, more, more, Go on! Throw 'em down yer neck! That's how we really got to see how E can get you like, tight out there. You've just got ter pelt it down yer. **1990**

We are that 'ard. That's why we'd never have girls in the band. Not playing instruments, anyway. Just to look dead sexy like, mebbe. Like them twenty birds we hired from the agency for the 'Kinky Afro' video. **1991**

I don't wanna get serious with music. Our music is about not even thinking about having a future. It's all going now. Right now, we are it. When it stops, it stops. We are just doin' what we are doin'. **1991**

Me old bloke, he works for us now, right. 'E's basically one of those working class geezers who never had a fookin' clue, always getting banged up or fucked over. Me mam was a nurse... she's like a three year old, really. Good woman and that but... she's a worrier... too nervous... Well you can't blame her with the phone going all the time and the police tellin' her that I've been booked and everything. But me old bloke instilled in me this belief that we may not be big 'ard blokes but there's not a situation we can't handle. And that's how we live our lives, for better or worse. **1991**

I mean I am in this for the fuckin' money, man. I was more interested in money than learning at school. Money, wearing the flashiest clothes and fookin' around. Naught's changed, really. We all wanna make a fuckin' pile. But at the same time I think we've got, like, principles... a fookin' sense of loyalty. We'd never leave Tony and Factory, like. Well, not unless someone offered us seven million or summat dead tasty like that. **1991**

E were great two years ago. I'd've legalised E. Yeah. No problem. But now, I don't know, like 'cos E... it can make ya nice an' mellow but it's also capable of doing proper naughty things to you as well. Proper bad naughty things to you. E can get you into big bother. Mind... drink's worse. But E and drink together's worse than that. Fuck, if we legalized E, man, we'd probably have a race of fookin' mutants on our hands. **1991**

America... I think it were good. I don't know if we were on one or if they were on one, man. There again, Americans are all fucking coke heads. Even the respect- able ones. We thought we'd sorted them all out, though. We thought we only met people who was great. We met people who said they were into Satan. We said, we are Satan, pal. **1991**

Gazza (Mondays drummer) insults everybody. He was running up to David Bowie all night in America going, 'He's a right fucking midget, he is'... mind, we did have some powerful draw out there. It was like smoking LSD. Took yer head off. Does that explain it? Naw. Gaz is just a right fooking cunt. **1991**

Bez has never been merely a dancer. He's not even on stage for people to look at. Bez is there for us. Just us. It was never to make the band look good... now the whole thing has blown up and he's a dancer. I'm a songwriter and we're

a band. Which is weird because all we wanted to do is fuck about. But things suddenly got big... It's a job, now. It has been for a while. If we didn't treat it as a job, people like you would never get pissed off with us never turning up and what not.

At one time we pleased ourselves. If we didn't feel like doing something, we just wouldn't do it. But we are aware that we have done that too much recently. I think we are growing up a little bit. Suddenly you begin to realise that people, journalists and that, are only really doing their jobs. You do learn to respect that a bit. I used to think they'd all be overawed meeting us... or underawed, or whatever. But that's not the case. We are just next the band along to them... which is fair enough. **1991**

Some people say we are weird because we are different from other bands. Because we talk a load of shite, sometimes, but those people don't know us, do they? We are not really weird. We're not in a daze. You can't be in a daze all the time, can ya? You gotta know what you are doing. We all know... and reality. What the fuck is that, man? I don't even think about that.

As far as I'm concerned, I'm not interested. I'm not interested in dying

people. I don't give a fuck about anyone else. I'm interested in me, my mates. I couldn't give a dong about anyone else. As far as I'm concerned, I want them to build loads of top space ships so we can start looking at proper planets and stop looking about, doing stupid things here... Actually, that's a dumb, horrible thing to say. If someone dying came up to me. I'd help them. But you really have to look after yourself and your mates. If a load of Ethiopians were dying in that park over there I'd do my best to help them. I'd have a go at it 'cos I don't like to see anybody like that. Especially families. But I'm not going to get into all that bollocks because I've not got time for it and it's just not my world. **1991**

I wouldn't say we were ahead of our time. I wouldn't go out and say that. I can say there is no one quite like us, when I know whose music we rip off. We rip off everybody. No exceptions. I can't tell you who, though, Paul Daniels doesn't give his secrets away, does he? Mind you, Tom O'Connor just did. Ha! Look at David Nixon! The bald bloke. You could always tell what David was up to. He was the old school, David. Three bottles of whisky and he didn't give a fuck.

Basically we don't know what the rules are supposed to be. I can't say we consciously go out to copy summat. We end up doing fings what are stored in our heads. We put it out our own way, like. If I was to copy a picture, any picture, then what I would do would look fuck all like the original. But I'd still be stealing in a way. That's what we do with songs.

See, lots of bands copy in a really obvious way. That's just fucking stupid because they just end up like some shite parody or something. To be really honest, we couldn't do it anyway. We tried. We were a copy band and our cover versions were shite. I sounded like the world's worst pub singer. So you have to have a bit of nous to get by. If that's fooling people, so what? Maybe it is. **1992**

We admire professionalism, man. Our attitude is that we just don't wanna do anything for anybody, if we don't wanna. If we are in a bad mood, we don't do the concert. It might be unprofessional but it can't be done, can it? None us of grew up with discipline. We can't get into it. Like these lads who come from the army on leave. They're going, "It's fucking great, man. The sarge made me stand on one leg in the corner for three hours with me hand behind me head and balancing a cherry on me nose". Well, I mean, what a dickhead. If they like discipline, that's

them. But there is no way any cunt would have me stood on one leg with a cherry on me nose, just 'cos the sarge said so. **1991**

If people want to think I'm Peter Sellers in the prime minister film, that's fine by me. What's it called? *Being There*. When they thought he wus a genius cos he didn't have a clue. Never been a film. Shit film that... meaning good. Shit means good in Manchester. Never been a film? That means it's great. It does get confusing, yeah. Never been confused. That means it's not confusing.

We are always talking backwards or forwards. Saying what we don't mean. Meaning what we don't say. Probably because we've done too many drugs. **1996**

Why drugs? Uh... well... illumination pal. Yeah! Illumination definitely. Well illumination like, half the time anyway. 'Cos the other half we just like to get fookin' roarin' shit faced, y'know wharrrasayin? **1990**

PCP is alright but it's dangerous gear. We had a good time on it but I can imagine fucking flipping out on it. It sent me a bit off me shed. I was trying to lift up cars, lift

up anything in fact. I remember walking down the street trying to snatch the gold off black kids. I should have been shot. **1991**

L.A. was different again. People hate it but I really loved it. Wouldn't mind moving there. Our hotel rooms were right around a pool and the jacuzzi. I've smoked some strong stuff but never like that Mexican weed we got. It was instant death. You had three pulls on it and you couldn't move your legs, you couldn't breathe. You were just sat there, dead. A cabbage, trapped inside your head and paranoid. We were gonna try and see Batman but I was gibbering at a million miles an hour. We've caned some bush in our time but nowt like that. That's why, when you see films of Mexicans, they are always slumped with their heads in their hands. It's the weed that does it. **1991**

To be really really honest, I always wanted to live a rock n' roll life but throughout the Mondays big thing, their big moments, I was heavily sedated by smack. All them big Wembleys and G-Mexs, I can't remember very well. Bits but not whole things. With the music it always seemed that other people got more excited by it than me. I was right into sex, drugs and rock 'n' roll but, for me, the rock 'n' roll always came last. **1996**

It happened to me a lot... not knowing where I was. I tell you, those Wembley dates. I know we did them, seen the reviews but I can't remember a single thing about them. And at Newcastle. Well, I was late for that Newcastle gig, very late. So I gets there and all these security guards are giving me double hassle and I just couldn't understand it. I kept saying, "Let me through, you bastards, I'm the lead singer." They looked a bit dubious for a while, nodding to each other, like, before they all seemed to agree and began clearing a way for me to get to the stage. I climbed on and remember feeling really shocked. The

place looked so plush and massive. Then it dawned on me that it wasn't our gig at all. It was Simply Red's venue down the road. **1996**

We didn't want to play at G-Mex at all. It just seemed like a load of hassle, the very idea of headlining such a place seemed, well it seemed like too much hard work. All of us gathered around and agreed, fucking hell, it would have to be like playing a small club, wouldn't it? We could get on, bash about for half-an-hour, fuck off and have a good time. That was always the Mondays. But G-Mex. Jeezus. We weren't U2 and we knew it. Eventually we relented. Fuck knows why... Oh, it was these two local lads, Jimmy and Muffy who handled our merchandising. They just said, "Do it lads, we will sell it for you, no problem. We'll get it sorted." So we did it... and, yes, it was a fucking hassle. At least, what I can remember of it. **1992**

Tony's (Wilson) got this thing about us. He thinks we are far more special than we actually are, y'know. All this shit about me being a genius... fuckin' hell Tony, come on, grow up for fuck's sake. I think he always felt a bit guilty, being a nice middle class grammar school boy and all that. I know that was why he was drawn into punk in the first place, partly to get away from all those poncy cunts at Granada. And he'd mix with, like kids on the dole, with no education and no future and he'd feel real at home. He'd get on really well with them and then feel mega-guilty 'cos of his fucking smart job at Granada and all that. And that's what we are to him. A sort of link to the street.

He loves us 'cos we are real but, fuck knows, he goes way over the top. Sometimes I feel like shakin' him, saying, fucking hell Tony, we are just a bunch of useless fucking tossers out on the fucking make. Trouble is, 'ed then say, "Yeah, I know, fantastic aren't you?" You can't fucking win really. Mind you... if we had all been to college – and I really wish I had sometimes – we'd be a really shit band, wouldn't we? **1992**

MONDAY, MONDAY...BEZ AND SHAUN IN PERFORMANCE

Rave On...
The Drugs Scene

I always said the better we got there's no way we'd be wasting our time on drugs. We only took drugs in the first place out of boredom. Even if you had a gram a day heroin habit, it was cheaper than going water skiing or windsurfing. **1991**

I'm not an alcoholic. I was a drug addict. My liver's a bit hard but all the damage that has been done to me's really by drugs and that can be repaired. If you're an alcoholic, you're finished. **1996**

I've stopped taking E. Last time I did, I was the last one out of the warehouse. Didn't know where I was. I had a load of E in my pockets 'cos I was sellin' 'em. I put about ten in my mouth to go out and they all melted. Sent me potty. I ended up having a heart attack on Oxford Road. Took me three weeks to recover. I couldn't even move the side of me body. Totally cabbaged. **1992**

Of course I sometimes want to hit people. Everybody does. Normal people do but what's normal, you know? It depends on how you feel. I did, last night, having antibiotics and booze. I wanted to run down the road fucking axing everybody, me. **1991**

Wouldn't that be a good fucking idea? (To give acid out in schools). Say, how do we know it's not going on? I mean, fucking hell! Controlling a lot of kids. I mean there's some drug that is supposed to make you really intelligent but you can't smoke dope with it. I mean, I was talking about getting into that. If I was bored like, and had loads of money and I was in a Morrissey situation, I'd well have a go at it. The thing all of us need at the moment, all of us would love to go for three months on our own private hospital on a beach. They'd have to work with us proper... not pop us full of pills and leave us in a fucking wheelchair. **1991**

I did *Top Of The Pops* straight. I wasn't pissed, I wasn't stoned or anything. People were saying, it's gonna be better when you're not stoned and you're not using the drug, and I did it. So I sing live and I forget all my words. I've done lots of shows all over the world where I've been stoned, I never forget me words. So I'm straight and I'm trying to keep myself together and everything and I fuck up. I was nervous. **1992**

A lot of what we said and what went down around then was simply to do with drugs. I can hardly remember any of it, anyway. There's a few little bits I can remember and bits of it are coming back, but mostly it's all a blur. The more I do remember the more embarrassed I get, so I generally try not to think about it. I don't think anything that I thought was really bad. We were just off our boxes, just daft lads. Didn't give a shit. Like, I called people a lot of names, caused a lot of problems but, really, it was just daft lads stuff. You see, we didn't give a fuck and, eventually, we got stitched up for it. **1993**

I don't want to go there... I know there will be people there I don't want to see, 'cos they will have drugs on them and that. **1993**

When you have a real problem with drink and drugs when you are in your twenties and you are still young and everything... fine, but when you see older people who are addicted, I think it looks double sad. It's like, 'kin hell, get some control. You are not exactly a young lad anymore so you have got to pull your socks up, get some control. I think you have got a responsibility to yourself but then maybe I'm a hypocrite.

Not everyone can be Keith Richards, drinking vodka for breakfast and shit like that. I'm not knocking Keith, I think it's

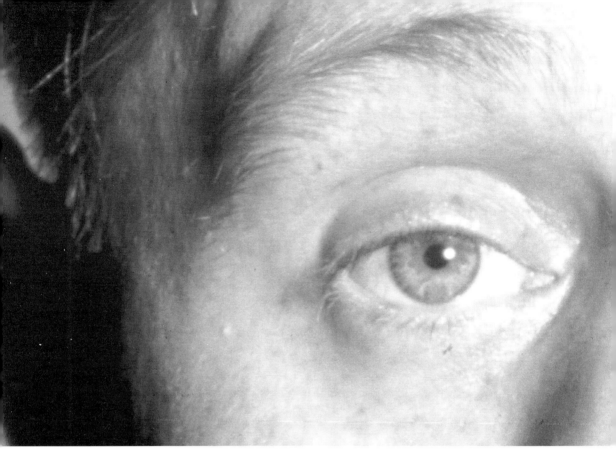

mega, but I don't see myself as being in any sort of league like that. **1993**

Drugs was the excuse they used when the Mondays broke up, but drugs didn't have nearly as much to do with it as people think. Three of the band had totally changed. It was all about money, one of them even wanted to consider pension plans. The easiest thing to do was to blame the drugs. But the drugs, the heroin, had always been there. When I walked out of the EMI deal it was because I thought the deal was shite. We had a meeting about breaking the band up and the guitarist (Mark Day), who's now working back at the post office, turned around and said, 'Well, your drug habits ..." And the rest of the band, even those I'd fallen out with, said "Fuck off, Mark, it's got fuck all to do with that." **1993**

I was buying a sixteenth of rock in the morning at eight o'clock, and I'd smoked that by dinner time and then I'd buy another sixteenth of a rock and at night time I'd buy an eighth of a rock. I was just buying sixteenths and eighths and just

smoking the fucker. Once you start smoking, it's terrible. It's the worst, dirtiest drug in the world. It's easily the cause of more problems than the smack. We kept the smack thing quite well under control for years. **1996**

I can honestly say that none of us have drug habits. None of us are dependent on drugs. I had a habit that I carried around for years but I've not had drugs for a while. I don't need them. I wouldn't change anything in the past, though. No way. We did what we set out to with the Mondays. I was the oldest, eighteen or nineteen and we had a couple of fifteen-year-olds in the band and all we wanted to do was live rock n' roll.

We didn't get into the music biz to discover drugs and fuck about with instruments. We wanted a rock n' roll life instead of doing shitty little things and getting a wanky job. We wanted to stay out of prison. So living rock n' roll was cool. When you are in your thirties and you have got habits and you're fucked, rock n' roll needs a break from you and you need a break from rock n' roll. **1995**

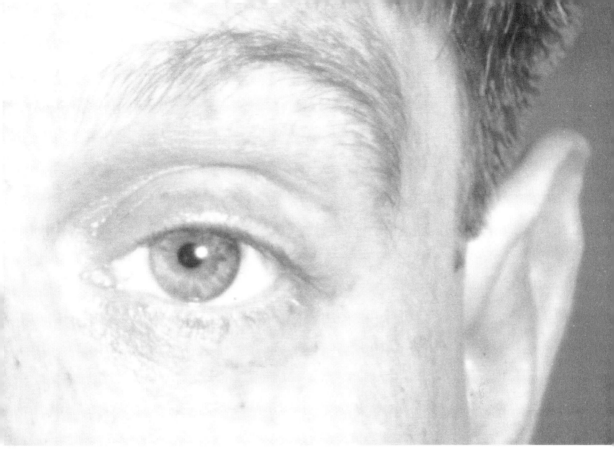

I'm 34. Ten years ago I was really ambitious and shit. I was out, Jimmy Corkhilling about. But from 24 to 34 a lot of shit's gone down. At 24 I never thought about the week ahead of me. Whatever was around that day, I had and did and never thought about tomorrow. The next day? You worried about it when it came. But when I got to 30 I knew it was grow up time. I really thought, I don't want to grow up to be like an alkie old man with me drugs. It freaked me out, big time. You get wiser, too. When you're young you've got your own opinion and that's it. If there's a question for me now, I'm like a computer. I go, brain, give me five possible solutions to this problem. And it goes ding, ding, ding and comes up with answers from all points of view. I don't just see both sides of things now, I see it in fucking 3D. **1996**

I took E on the last Grape UK tour. I had a good night. My body will not take E like it used to though. All these kids are going out and they have a pill and then another pill. I mean, they've got to remember you've got to slow down with these

things. Take half of one, test it before you start eating them like fucking toffee. **1996**

It's been four years since the Mondays split up and there was a period of two years where I didn't touch any drugs . Like I say, I'm no angel and I'm still no angel. I've had a blast in the last twelve months. The thing with me is, especially close people, they see you when you've had a smoke and they get worried about you, like it's all going to start to pile up again. I've got to be really, really careful, especially in Manchester. It's just like Disneyland for drugs. I'm not turning round and saying that I'm one hundred percent strong . If I have a few too many drinks and I'm in the centre of town, it's just so easy for me to get a bag of goodies. Then it's easy for me to say I don't give a fuck. I'm alright. I just constantly keep smoking weed because it keeps the urges from me. **1997**

When I hit thirty I still had a habit and I'd been wanting to get away from it for a while. I didn't celebrate my birthday or

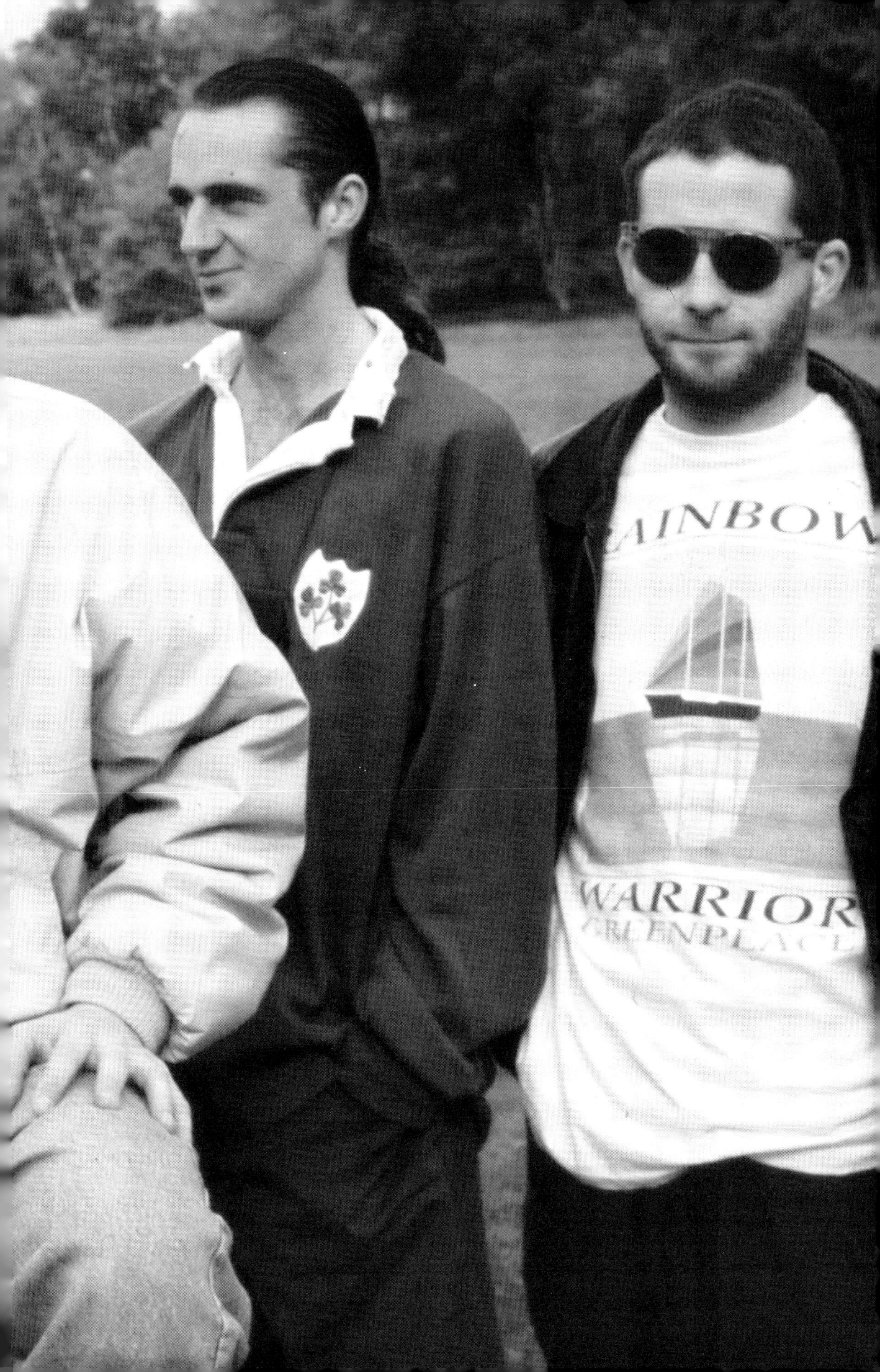
WARRIOR

nothing, man. I was pretty down with myself. So I got on the Prozac and within eight weeks, it was like someone had took me brain out, washed it, given it a rub down, blown all the cobwebs off and put it back in. **1997**

After 14 years... I decided to come off junk. Four years ago I was on the methadone for 12 months. Huge doses to begin with. And some of that time I was using heroin on top of the meth, which was making it double hard. I ended up coming down to a very small amount of meth, but it was getting me in the mind, that's what I could never handle. So I went on Valium and then Prozac. Prozac is what helped me get off the gear.

If I hadn't taken that drug, man, fuck knows where I'd be now. It's what allowed me the will power. I could actually say to myself, 'come on, you can do it'. Desperation helped, but Prozac gives you back your will power, man, but eventually it's down to you. I didn't really have much of a choice. Ya see, we had always done whatever we wanted to. Do music. Do drugs. Sell drugs. Get stoned. Have a laugh, really. So when I wanted to come off smack, I did. I wanted to and I did. Like I can't use the excuse that I'm a mad little bastard kid anymore.

A lot of my family have died through drugs and alcohol. I see people around Manchester in their thirties and forties, fucking sad, spotty drug-addicted old men. And I don't want to be one of those fuckers. And whether it's brew or skag, you do become that sort of bloke. **1997**

I didn't stop taking smack for health reasons. If I'd been drinking vodka for the rest of me life instead I'd be in a far worse way than if I'd carried on taking skag. You can go to all the clinics in the world, you can go cold turkey, come off on meth or whatever, but you aint gonna stop unless you really want to... I've got it in perspective, now. I can do a trip or some jellies and it's just a quick trip to Disneyland y'know? That's because you've now got something else in your life. **1997**

Oh yeah, he's a dude man (Michael Hutchence). Danny (Producer and writing collaborator) who is more Black Grape than anybody... er what was I sayin? Oh yeah, Michael Hutchence... er, sorry that skunk has knocked me out. Yeah, well, you see Danny doesn't like to be doing just one thing, right, so... sorry man, forgotten what I was talkin' about... Oh yeah right, Michael... er Danny did some work for Michael after I recommended him and after that we got together. He's a top bloke. A rock n' roll geezer. I mean, I was never into INXS. I remember Gaz from The Mondays, who always used to be dead into this long hair poser look... fook! Skunk man... what was I talkin' about? **1997**

Oh yeah, what happened, right, I was comin' out of the Brat Awards, totally fookin' bladdered and I got in a car with a load of Scousers. We pulled up at this gaff where some, er, cannabis resin could be procured. Anyway, it turns out this house is being watched, innit, So we turned up and the bizzies are right up our arse. They get out the car and I says, 'I've got fook all on me.' And the next thing I know there's this bag on the seat where I've been sat, because one of the Mickey's (Scousers) tossed his bag of Charlie into the car, and I got nicked. Lucky though, I didn't have any coke in me blood, so nowt came of it. And I left me mobile phone and me award with one of the lads. Then *The Sun* ran a piece sayin' I made it all up and I'd been seeing some bird so, of course, Oriole goes bally! But *The Sun* printed an apology so that was that. Pretty mad night, though. **1997**

I'm not going to encourage, (daughters, to take drugs) no. Hopefully my kids will have something of me in them anyway. This safety catch I have. No matter what you say about me, I know when it's time to bale out. It's a natural cut off switch. **1997**

Fucking hell! Let's at least start them with marijuana before Ecstasy, for Christ's sake. I wouldn't push anything on them, but if they want to try and experience something, it's their life. **1997**

I'm not going to encourage my kids to take drugs... but I've been around children who've grown up around weed being smoked and I've seen them grow into adults and they are a lot more sensible than the one's who haven't. Hopefully if any of my kids have got anything of me and their mother in them... well, I might be known as a fucking lunatic but I've still got common sense. I'm still pretty responsible. **1997**

In my pockets now... let's have a look. I don't know what that pill is. I found it in a jacket pocket. That's a grand and there's about two ton there, so that's twelve hundred quid, two Uzi bullets, half a cigarette, some skunk weed, two packets of Rizlas, an elastic band, and there's no tinfoil on me. **1997**

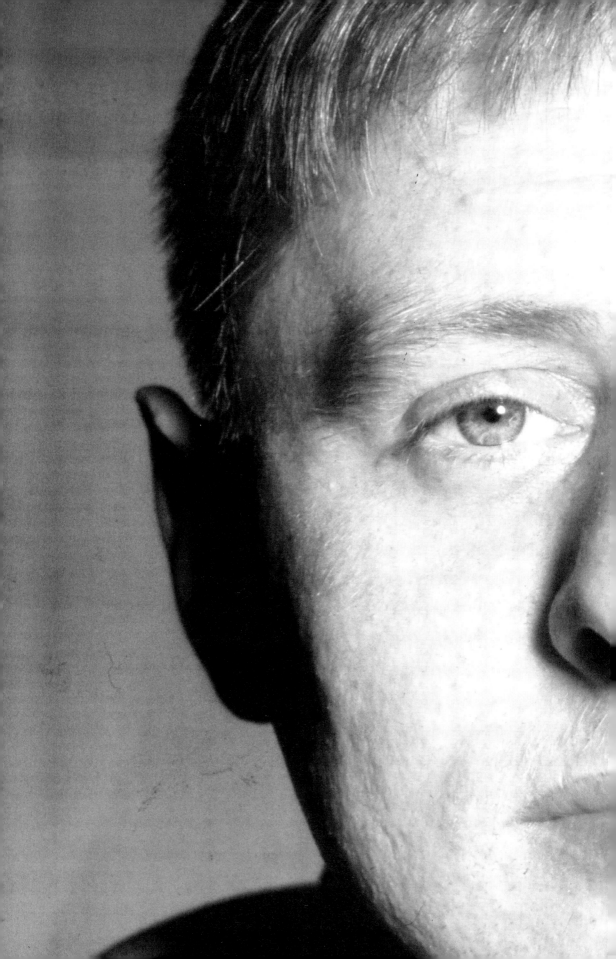

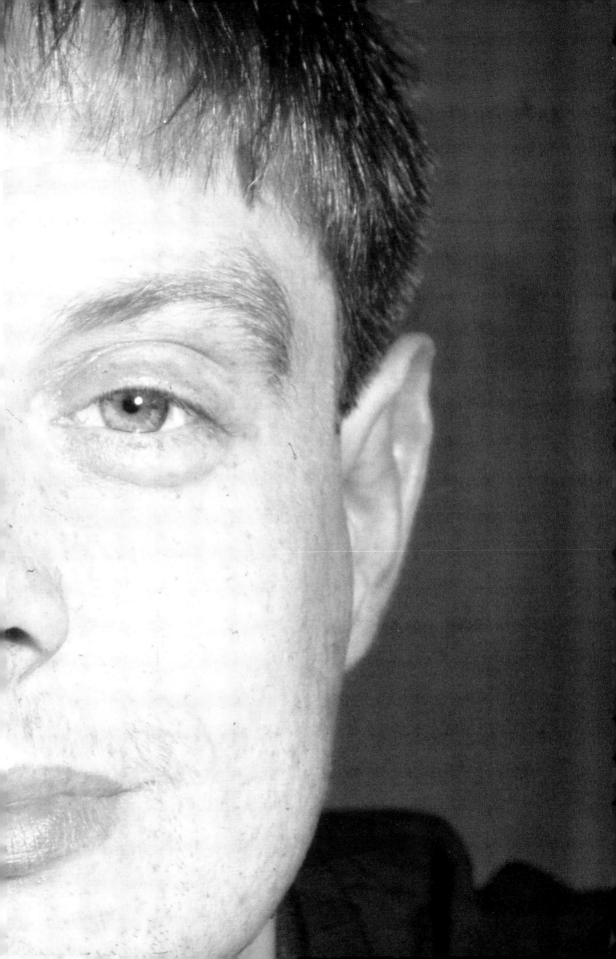

Cut 'Em Loose Bruce... Goodbye To The Mondays

Bez wrote three cars off in three weeks. We keep lending him cars, man, and he keeps writing them off. Honda Prelude, Golf GTI... and he's not even passed his test. **1991**

It was just us, man, just being mad fucking bastards. It's his fucking mouth, man, and me just doing stupid stuff. But we was always clever bastards you know. Bez was always pretty sussed, even when he was out of it. Me and him, we did all the fucking leg work in the Mondays. In fact, if we had been totally straight we'd probably have found a couple of dickheads like us to work for us. Fuck man, if we had been straight we'd have ended up managing us. But you know me and Bez. It's his fucking mouth, the cack we talk, the daft shit we do. His mouth and the way he looks, well, it just gave us a certain rep. That's that. **1993**

It's just one big fucking joke, we should be getting really serious but we can't. I don't think we'll ever get our heads together to be that serious. We've been trying but when your manager is a bigger fucking idiot than you are, it's difficult. **1991**

We had to choose an Elektra artist to cover and the obvious one was Tom Waits, 'cos we are all double Waits fans. I think it would have been really cool but then someone, can't remember who it was, came up with this John Congos track, 'He's Gonna Step On You Again'. I vaguely remembered it from being, like, dead young. We knew it would be great. In fact the John Congos song had been a mere afterthought, slapped onto the back of a tape full of Tom Waits and Doors songs sent over from Elektra. It wasn't, after all, regarded as one of Elektra's finest moments. **1991**

I wrote 'Loose Fit' when the Gulf War 'ad just started. We were in America and kept hearing bits on telly about Air Force bases and bombin' raids. Was I interested in the war? Yeah, of course, but I wasn't concerned about it. I didn't give a fook. I just thought it was great TV. I fookin' loved it. **1992**

I suppose 'Rave On's about a group of lads on the town for a good night and all bowlin' into a fucking club. And when I said, "Are you Man U?" At Elland Road, I wasn't just asking the crowd if they supported Man United, I was taking the piss out of the Leeds fans 'cos they come up to you and say, "Are you Man U?", even if you've got Man U tattooed on your fuckin' head. Then they get their knife out and give yer a fookin' slash. **1992**

I wrote 'God's Cop' thinkin' about James Anderton, but there was no real reason for that. I didn't have any big axe to grind. He was just an easy subject. I find songwriting easier now that I'm writing for a movie because I've got themes to write about. I'm writing songs now for this film, Baby Bighead about money and power, 'cos that's what the film's about. I can identify with it, the idea of going from having nothing to a world of money and cars and fookin' travelling everywhere...**1991**

Now 'Bob's Yer Uncle' is a dirty sex song. We were in the studio and Oakey (Paul Oakenfold) said, "C'mon lads, let's have a fookin' sexy one". But I can't write a proper sexy song. It just comes out like schoolboy, pervy stuff. I don't know why that is. **1991**

Judge Fudge... it's just a word, innit? Judge Fudge! Judges are like perverts in wigs, judge fudge tickle judge fudge tickle... they're all fucking perverts... Yeah, well, most of them. I'd say they were perverts in wigs. We know that goes on, I'm not saying all of them but most of them are Judge Fudge tickle. I'm not saying they shouldn't be allowed to wear the fucking wigs. I'm not saying they shouldn't dress as women. I'm not saying anything. Just Judge Fudge. Nanananana. **1991**

I'm really proud of how everybody in our band are friends and still get on. To keep that, I'm quite willing to split the band after this tour for two years and let us all get out and try different things. **1991**

Working with Oaky and Osborne was right for the time but now it's time to move on. I couldn't see us doing another 'Pills'n'thrills' type of thing, but then we've always done exactly what we wanted. I mean anyone who would do a fuckin' stupid song like... er... what was the one we did with Karl Denver called? Yeah, right, 'Lazyitis'. Now that's a really lame and dumb song but that's what we liked about it. That's why we came out with it because it reflected what we like at the time. **1992**

I went to the Carter clinic in London, they have a 12 point plan for recovery from heroin, don't they. And one of the terms is that you've got to recognise, 'a being more powerful than yourself.' When I got there it was like, 'Oh God', 'Thank God' and things like that. And I thought it was a bit off-putting for people who have come to get off drugs, to have to go through all the God thing. But that said, your Grandma or someone you respect can be your God. It was like being brainwashed. At first I was fighting it. I'd been in rehabs before and it never works out 'cos I'd always left before the psycho-therapy started. This time, I had a go at it. I thought, well, brainwash me then. **1993**

One thing, a songwriting thing came out of the clinic thing. 'Stinkin' Thinkin''. That means all the thoughts you are thinking when you are getting straight. You are not supposed to think any bad thoughts, what you have said to people or things that you have done because they start playing over in your mind. It doesn't help, something good had to come out of the experience of being in there for a month, so it was them few words. **1993**

I had a great time in Barbados. Letting off steam and everything. I mean, all right, a few mad things happened and everything and when I came home I was whacked because we'd been on the big adventure theme park for a month. I was on a real holiday buzz, had a big, erm, party. Y'know, got totally fuckin' kettled. But I got myself straightened out and I was in the mood then to write some words, get into being into the music, get the tunes making me groove. **1992**

To us it's as simple as writing good tunes and having fun. Well, it should be that simple but then sometimes all the business shit gets in the way of it. I mean, yeah, I feel responsible to... like... no, I don't even feel responsible... I don't know what it is.
   We're all really close to each other, so if the lads give me a good track with some good bits that turn me on, I want to do well for them. I mean, I wanna get some lyrics out they like. For nobody else, just for them. I mean, I don't know if you have noticed but our band are really good friends, apart from Mark Day. After ten years his views are totally different from the rest of the band. We don't see it as much of a business or a pressure like he does. The five of us still treat it like a joke, like a laugh. I mean, OK, I went mad in Barbados or whatever and the rest of it, but the rest of the band are like, "Oh X went mad and now he's back to normal, it's sweet." **1992**

We've all got confidence in each other because to us friendship is more important than anything. The rest of the band are really supportive. We are just into getting our act together. **1993**

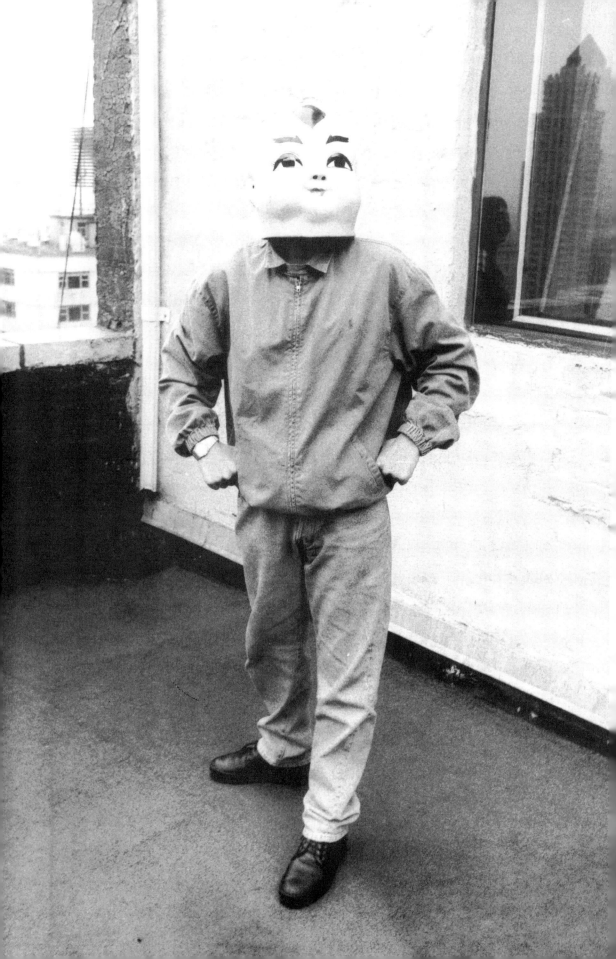

A Mondays' donation to the Hard Rock Cafe? Difficult one that. Maybe we should send a bong made from a Boddingtons beer can, a packet of Rizla, some tinfoil, an empty skag packet and the sheet me and Bez slept on when we shared a flat together. We never washed it, never changed it, must look like a Jackson Pollock painting. **1992**

Yes Please? It was a fucking disaster from beginning to end. We went over there (to Barbados) so I could stay off the smack 'cos they don't have smack over there. So the first thing that fucking happened was that I dropped me methadone in the fucking airport, three fucking gallons of methadone in a big fuckin' container. It was madness, there was these geezers running into the shop, finding any container they could to rescue the methadone. You know, scooping it up, glass and all. I had crunchy fuckin' methadone. So when we got over there we had to filter it all through this really strong linen. Anyway I'd set off with about 120 mil which I drank the moment I got to Barbados, 'cos by that time I was on 120 mil a day. That's a lot of fucking gear. **1993**

Fortunes man, we spent fortunes recording that fucking album. And that was just the recording of it. We spent a fortune all the fuckin' time. We always had money to be getting along with but we never actually made a bean. We spent the fuckin' lot. Like we spent three fuckin' months recording a little fucking noise for one of the tunes on that stupid fucking record. A month working out what it should sound like and two months recording it. I never liked it. I just wasn't interested at the time. I wasn't writing. I didn't give a fuck... No one really gave a fuck. They (the other Mondays) weren't interested in what I had to say and I didn't give a fuck about what they had to say.

   With the last Mondays' album everyone hated each other so bad it was fucking impossible to talk. It was like, 'I play the drums, so fuck off'. 'I play the fucking keyboards so fuck off'. 'I play the guitar so fuck off'. It just got so fucking obnoxious. It turned into the total fucking opposite of what we'd started out doing in the first place. You know in the early days we all had input, I could say, 'Try this, do that, whatever'. And we'd try loads of different stuff. That's what made The Mondays what they were. But by the time we came to record that last thing, we were all off on our own little trips. Even when we were playing live we weren't playing as a band, we were playing as fucking individuals. **1995**

Obviously, certain people started thinking about money, money, money all the time and once you start thinking like that... it all blows apart. **1993**

For a good few years we had good fun, me and Mark Berry made the music business interesting, turned it into a black comedy. But people didn't want fucking fun, so fuck it. It's no skin off my nose. It just used to get on my tits when there would be three million people who'd buy *The Sun* one week because somebody had done something or shot someone, then they would be saying to us, "Why did you say the band is splitting up?". As if that's really fucking important. Well, a few thousand people have been shot to fucking death (a reference to Yugoslavia), it all seemed fucking stupid to me. **1994**

We could have carried on. But our time had ended. It ended for the people in the band and that's it. I mean, what do they say? You turn into your father. Well, the rest of the band turned into Mark Day's father. It was just old and finished. **1994**

A Mondays' reunion. You'll have to ask the guitarist if he can get time off from his Post Office job. **1994**

I haven't got any ego problems. It's not like 'Oh I was a singer in a big band but now I'm a has-been so I need to get my head back in a magazine.' Anyway, anything I do now is going to get taken the wrong way. **1994**

The reason I haven't done anything recently or don't want to do anything is I'm still pretty bitter about the whole Factory thing. So, you know, I'd rather just forget it all for a while until I'm ready... until I'm not angry. **1993**

We, the Mondays, were supposed to be the worst of Thatcher. Well, maybe we fuckin' were. I mean, we listened to her. Of course we did, we listened to every fuckin' word and said, 'Right, you bitch, we'll take you at your word'. I've got to cheer the bitch, 'cos she got me off my arse. **1993**

Obviously people weren't even listening to the music. It just seemed like loads of people were signing bands and then, ten minutes later, deciding to drop them. They didn't even listen to the fucking bands. They just wanted to make lots of money. It was like the Stock Exchange. Buy Manchester, buy, buy, buy... Okay... Sell, sell, sell. **1993**

When I'd stopped the gear, it was the first time in years that I hadn't needed to be stoned to do anything. I was double straight. But as soon as the Mondays finished there was a lot of shit that had to be cleared up. Everyone fucking legged it. I was left to be responsible for a lot of things. Frozen assets and all that. But for me it was the best time I'd had in a long time. People used to come up to me and say, You've blown it, man. You fucked up the Mondays. I'd just fucking laugh. **1996**

Oh everyone hated us by then. We weren't getting written about any longer. We were getting written off. They all wanted to see us in the dustbin, man. They wanted to see us dead. **1996**

I think we have ripped the music industry off more than they have ripped us off. In the Mondays I didn't bother about what money was doing this and what money was doing that. We're meeting half the arseholes in this business and I was skagged up. I just used to go, 'Aw fuck it, man.' Going through all that definitely helped. The Mondays wasn't about making records... it was about living the rock 'n' roll life and getting out of our boring little existence. And we did. People used to come up to me after the band had split and say, 'You're a knobhead, you blew it'. And I'd think, what the fuck do you know? I was a £17 a week post boy. **1993**

The band was just money, money money in the end. They didn't have any interest in the music anymore. They thought they could just get this EMI deal, get two million, just go and sit back on the couch and make an album. Make a totally shit album. People say that my heroin habit split the band up. I had a perfectly healthy heroin habit before the Mondays were even going. It was only when everyone else started smoking crack that they got all these great ideas about how important they were. **1993**

I have no contact with them (the Mondays) now, apart from Bez and our kid. Did you notice, though, that straight after the band ended everyone out of the Mondays was saying, 'I've joined a band.' None of them have done dick. All the ones that have done the talking have done nothing. **1996**

I have got no anger or animosity about that (the Mondays' demise) at all. It was fun and classic rock 'n' roll or whatever. No, it's cool. I've got over all that. I am certainly ready to realise that, yeah, they always thought I was wrong and always thought they was fucking wrong, but I will say that it was a bit of both... **1997**

The Life & Times Of Black Grape... It's Great When You're Straight, Yeah!

After the Mondays... no I didn't have a perm. I had grown my hair long again, the same cut that Liam's got now, sort of thing. I had a big fucking 'I Am The Walrus' moustache. Just being a bit trendy two years before everyone. **1996**

I admit I'm a top bullshitter. But we all used to act. How the fuck do you think we got on with all the people in the record business? You see, all we ever wanted to do was get out of our shitty little fuckin' holes in Manchester. And whatever we had to say or do to get that, we did and said.
   I said a lot of crap. But I always have. All that shite about not wanting to be in a band an' all that. It was just me talkin' total cack again. The fuckin' truth is that, within a fortnight of the split, I was on a plane to New York sortin' out this lot (Black Grape). It took a lot of time to get a deal and stuff. And we had to get our shit sorted out. I had nothing. Not a fuckin' bean and, yeah, before anyone asks, I did get really fuckin' fat and grow an 'orrible moustache. **1995**

What we did with this album (*'It's Great When You're Straight, Yeah!'*), we wanted to do a sort of *Pin Ups* thing. Stick all sorts on. And we did have fun doing it, proper fun. That's what we are into, fun. We had a lot more swearing on it but we 'ad to cut it out. But it's not an angry record. In fact I think it's a good fuckin' laugh. Comic strip.
   Besides a couple of fuckin' tracks it's all pretty up. We wanted to make it fun. We wanted the stupid stuff in there as well. Like we recorded enough songs for two albums, but a lot of the really serious stuff we left off. And this fuckin' record only took us a few weeks to do. We just

do it. No way would we spend ages in the studio, man. Not now. We can come up with all sorts of shit all fuckin' day. Fuckin' rock n' roll, fuckin' 'ardcore, the tunes just keep fuckin' comin'. It's just like having a conversation. We buzz off each other man... it's dead easy. It's not like working, when we write, we just sit around talkin' the same old cack like when we were sittin' in Dry Bar. **1995**

Me and Kermit, we work upside down, inside out, back to front. We lay down rhythm tracks and then we get blitzed on weed. And then we start jokin and tryin' to make each other laugh. That's how we did the intro to 'Kelly's Heroes'... You know, the 'Jeesus was a black man/nah Jeezus was Batman...' That was just a conversation we had, then one of us went, "Hey... hang on a minute..." That's how it is, so don't go looking for any hidden depths, mate 'cos there ain't any. But that's how it is with the best stuff. It is spontaneous, kind of makes itself up as it goes along and becomes something else. Like all that Beefheart stuff. *'Trout Mask'*, man... fucking top record that. An' all these hippies would spend a decade tryin' to work the fucker out. It meant fuck all... and it meant everythin'. That's art innit. **1995**

I was singing that line, 'Go put your Reeboks on, man, and go play fucking tennis' at *Top Of The Pops* rehearsals and, it were funny 'cos I kept expecting to be told to change it and no one seemed to say anything. So I thought, well, they'll cut it out somehow, but they didn't. And nobody really cared. If you had done that ten years before, idiots would have kicked TV screens in, wouldn't they? **1995**

SHAUN RYDER... IN HIS OWN WORDS

To be honest, me mam were a bit made up about all that stuff with the Pope being upset about our lyric. First of all, it weren't half as worryin' as some of the other stuff that had been in the papers about me and, more importantly, all her neighbours' kids are into thievin' and that. So to have her son in trouble with the Pope, that's quite impressive for a Catholic. Not many folk can say the Pope knows Who yer son is, can they? **1995**

The first Black Grape album, recording it didn't exactly help our attempts to stay clear of the old chemicals. When we started recording it was just doing a bit of skank and that. But things soon began to harden a bit. I suppose we started to feel the pressure. That's the killer with this business. Suddenly you find you are in a position where you have it all to do and to cope you begin to slide into... well, you know. Things started to get a bit naughty again as that record was proceeding and we started partyin'. But after that I straightened up a bit. Not even any Charlie, or anything. **1996**

We only ever did two cover versions in the Mondays and, in the end it all comes down to whether the song's got a groove to it. Like 'Stayin' Alive' had a fucking groove to it, and there's nothin' that can top that. It's like when old punk and new wave came along, everyone was so paranoid they wouldn't admit they liked The Bee Gees and they were fucking top. Now wearing flares and liking disco is as punk as you can get. All the people who were slagging The Bee Gees were fucking idiots, man. But if we did a cover version now it would be 'My Mind's Playing Tricks On Me' by The Geto Boys... top fucking tune alright. **1996**

I haven't enjoyed myself so much in... er... I don't think I have ever enjoyed being on TV so much. I hope the little thirteen-year-olds all watched it. If the thirteen-year-olds want to see the show, they'll get to see it no matter how late it's on. I used to watch things like *The Old Grey Whistle Test* when I was a kid. You just do. I don't give a fuck how old a kid is, he'll watch it if he wants to. I was eight and I knew The Sex Pistols were coming on the telly. I'd kick up a stink. I'd have to watch it. *Later* is a live show and we've just played a live show, tonight and people were there to see it. And with people like Gregory Isaacs watching as well, it's a top buzz. **1995**

Yeah, I'm fucking pleased to be on *Later* because it's a fucking top show. I think the important thing is that Jools is presenting it and he's a top guy. A real musician. Because he's on, and everybody sits around watching everybody else's performance, it just makes the atmosphere really good, no question. And it's better than most of the shit that gets on telly these days. **1995**

Our songs come straight outta me record collection. We just twist it and distort it and fuck it up until no one recognises it and we can't get sued for it. Other records are usually the trigger. **1996**

When we did the video for 'Reverend Black Grape', I had this beautiful Comme Des Garcons jacket in me bag and some fucker nicked it. You try telling the insurance people that you had that and a Gaultier jacket which cost a couple of grand each and a pair of trousers that cost £120 and a nice Stone Island thing that was £600 and they don't fucking believe you. You only end up getting, like, three grand back, cunts. **1996**

Kermit's mother was upset at the time, he has been making his mother cry since the womb. It made no difference to Kermit. He just said 'sorry' and then went out and scored again. Other people can't make a difference. Not when you are like that. **1995**

It's getting sorted now (failing to get American visas for Black Grape) and hopefully we'll be over in February. It was pretty obvious we weren't getting in because all the other times we've gone over to the States, we had the old black passports with no bar-code and you don't say, "Yes I've done this, I've done that." You lie. But with the new ones your record comes up on the screen from Interpol or somewhere and ours goes DRUGS DRUGS DRUGS DRUGS. But it's getting sorted now. Fuckin' ironic really, not getting into America because of fucking drugs. Like it's a really drug-free easy-going sort of place. Like we might corrupt them. Makes you laugh, don't it? **1996**

Eventually we got into America. I got put on review and they let me in. Kermit they didn't let in because what they like to see before they will let you in the States is that you've done a bit of rehabilitation. Now Kermit's never done any rehab, neither's Bez. It's down on my forms that I've done some rehab and shit like that, so in the end I was allowed right through. **1996**

Making the Black Grape album, the vibe was excellent. It shows on the album. I think you can tell that we had a really good time making it. The vibe of this band is great because we haven't been together like a husband and wife team for twelve years. We're all fresh and still shagging each other. We are not having to. It's still like having a fresh chick. And we're clean. **1996**

Bez is family. Bez is free to come and and go as he pleases with our band. When we were recording Bez was down there and it's like, "C'mon B, come back onstage." So it started off being fun again but nine months later, when they are expecting him to do interviews and the dude ain't getting paid, you see how he's getting fucked off. They won't even give him his train fare, he has to ask for it. He's on strike. It's not a question of whether he'll be back. He'll never be away as far as I'm concerned. **1997**

Well obviously people thought, Kermit and Shaun, drug nutters. They'll either end up junkies or dead. But what they never understood is that we love making music more than we ever loved getting

out of it. With the Mondays that wasn't the case. We started playing music because we wanted that rock n' roll lifestyle, the music came second. Me and Kermit always got the music together even if we was getting out of it every now and again. And we are keeping it together now, better than ever. **1997**

I was just getting back to normal, chilling with Oriole in Mexico and I had to go and catch a fucking bug, didn't I? Dodgy fucking Mexican food poisoning, dude. The worst. 'Cos after the tour we just had, I had to fuck off. Kermit's in hospital with septicaemia, caught it off dirty water, didn't he? They've got him down the isolation with all the AIDS patients and if he'd left it any longer he'd be dead. Bits of his heart flaking off, bits of his liver flaking off. **1996**

I remember thinking, 'fookin' hell, me mate's (Kermit) in a bad way'. We just wanted him to get better. Didn't have time to be thinkin' about ourselves. But now, believe it or not, I am pretty easy at the moment. My favourite thing at the moment is. like, just having a beer and a bit of weed. I don't really wanna do any-thing else. I just wanna concentrate on the music. I can do without caning it. Anyway, skunk's enough for anyone. **1996**

It's everything, dude, we take the best from everything. We love all types of music, whether it's rock, hip hop... opera... of course I love opera. I love to listen to bits of it. I mean, I couldn't have it on all day, like I couldn't listen to fucking thrash all day either, but I cer-tainly like little bits. **1997**

Most of Black Grape don't go off on wild parties, shagging loads of chicks or anything. Basically there's me, Kermit and Danny who are a bit rock n' roll. That's it. But we are not this big, boozing, partying, drugging thing. Alright, I've had my fucking problems with drugs and I like to get stoned, but that's about it. The rest of the people in this band are pro musicians. **1997**

One of the reasons we cut shit out (from *The Grape Tapes* video) is because, even when we are joking about things, it sounds like we are being very serious and evil. Even when I'm making a joke about the cunt from the *Manchester Evening News*, saying, 'I'll get his legs broken', fucking hell dude, it's a joke. **1997**

The future of Black Grape is I've got two more albums on my contract. The thing is, I really do like working with Danny and Kermit and I think I've definitely got at least another good album in me. I always want to be involved in music, but I'm 35, two more albums will take me up to being 40. It's not disrespecting anybody, but I really don't want to be on-stage and touring at 40 years old. Maybe I'll change my mind, but I just don't know what happens after 40. **1997**

It took us eight weeks to do the new album ('*Stupid, Stupid, Stupid*'). Some bands take that long to do a single. We were completely in charge. That was the big difference between the last album and this one. Because, then we had, say, 60% control. This time it was total. After three months off I was feeling good, everyone was in a good mood, everyone wanted to work with each other, so I said, if we are all in the right frame of mind, let's get in there and do it. **1997**

(On music and the music business) I couldn't give a fuck. I couldn't give a flying sheep's dick about music, jingly jangly bollocks. I don't feel responsible for fuck all. I make music. I don't listen to Lush or Loop. That letter... who's that letter off? It ain't off a real fucking person who has to graft. Fucking reads-the-music-papers-knobhead. Real people I know never even bought the *NME* years ago. They had more real things to be getting on with than buying fucking music papers and worrying about jingly jangly! **1992**

Sometimes like... I'm sitting on a train or something, just chillin', doing a bit of the old people watching. And I see some

cunt sit down... some student cunt and he's sitting there reading his *NME* or *Melody Maker*. He could be reading about us... or not, it doesn't matter because it starts me thinking and, round and round my head are all these thoughts. Like why is that cunt wasting his fucking time reading the *NME*? Why is he listening to shit like Happy Mondays, he's supposed to be intelligent for fuck's sake. All these brainy people, all fucking sitting around reading the fucking music press. I mean... I know they have to relax but what a fucking waste of energy if you think about it.

Shit I do... sometimes... I love music, live for it but then again, that's all I've ever 'ad. It were either that or carry on in the fucking postal service. But what about some cunt who is training to be a lawyer. I'll have his fucking money and that but, fancy him fucking listening to us. What a prick! What started me thinking like this? Oh yeah, it was in Oxford... or was it Cambridge? Somewhere like that and they are all running around in Mondays or Inspirals T-shirts. In one sense it's fantastic, that dickheads like us can make some kind of influence over their lives. But then again, maybe it just proves that they are no better, they are just as fucking stupid as us. Just as fuckin' gullible... or maybe they see us as exotic. A bit of rough. Fuck knows... mad innit? **1992**

Everyone at *Top Of The Pops* was laughing at Daniel O'Donnell and for me he was the best thing on the show that week. He was a proper pro. The Inspirals did a good job but, I'll tell you, that man was a real pro. He the old grafting type singing geezer innee? And he still sings it like he loves it. **1992**

I don't know whether it was because of the Mondays and all the shit involved with that, or whether it was just part of the ageing process. I went through a phase where I practically hated all modern music, didn't want to be fucking doing with it and, worse, certainly didn't want anything to do with the music business. In fact I'd loathe people who mentioned it, who still found it interesting. I think it was a reaction, a kind of defence, but, all of a sudden it all seemed so fucking stupid.

So I thought well, Shaun, get away from it a bit. Trouble was, other people told me that they had the same experience even though they weren't in a band. So I reckon its a natural thing... but, fucking hell. There's a lot more to life, isn't there? **1994**

Music business. It bores the twat off me. **1993**

Success doesn't fuck you up. It's the people you are involved with who fuck you up. **1994**

Rock 'n' roll is a good way to have a good time. A decent life. It's better than being in the army. Except you get to kill people in the army. **1996**

(On the Music Press) Yeah... until a load of snotty little kids start writing for the music papers. I just think some of the kids who write for such magazines should have a smack on the head and be told they can't write on their own, without stabilisers, until they are 22. 'Til they start appreciating music, whether it's Frank Sinatra or Interstella. It's all music, it's music. And then you get some snotty kid writing in some magazine sayin' this is great, he's into this now and in one year's time he's slagging off what he was into. There's not enough people liking music for what it is.

I don't need my dick sucked by the media or anybody else. I don't need to get involved with the music business, the press or anybody in England. I haven't done anything lately but I believe in this band (Interstella) and its music. **1993**

I'll tell you, I have never regarded myself as being hip, or any of that shit. All that means, when someone is regarded hip, is that they are part of a big stupid fucking gang. Just fucking sheep. Like one of those bands who sound like a load

of other bands and they all sort of stick together, make it together and then all go out of fashion at once. I never feel sorry for them cunts because they decided, at some point, to take the easy route. To sit on some fucking band wagon, like all of a sudden, we had all these baggy type bands. It was really stupid too, 'cos there was some really good bands in there, with that lot. Mind you, if I think about it, perhaps I can't blame them. You don't get many chances in life, do you.

Funny thing though, I've never found it necessary to think in those terms. I've always done natural things... like all the music the Mondays grew up listening too, maybe some was hip and maybe a lot of it wasn't. Never fucking gave it a thought. Funkedelic to fucking Showaddywaddy... I mean, they all had their fucking place. They all sank into me fucking head. All music is good... even shit music has its place. **1993**

(On the Factory collapse) You've got to think about it in the right way. From 1987 onwards there were no albums out on Factory, right. Electronic didn't 'shift units' as they say. New Order hadn't done dick. We made all their money for them. We took them from a small building to a big building. I personally filled their club for them. Their club was empty until our little gang got on it and turned it from being a hundred people off their heads on E to, like, two and a half thousand or whatever fits in there.

At the time, we're telling Tony why do you keep putting forty grands and fifty grands into these bands that have got to go round the loop? Where did that money come from? That's coming out of our money. But I've kept me mouth shut for three years and let him say that I brought Factory down and it's all bullshit. Even on a bog wall in America someone had written 'Shaun Ryder has ruined Factory'. I thought that was really funny, man. **1996**

When I did that Interstella thing, people said I was just tryin' to get back into the scene. But I was just doing it for a favour. Those were the best two years of my life, just chillin' out. People used to come up to me and say, 'Feel sorry for yer, man, yer blew it.' And I was fuckin' mega. And I was still a smackhead then, of course. **1994**

I'm not name dropping but I was over in New York at the weekend with, like, Keith and Ronnie and that and we was hanging out and they still love going out and playing fucking music. I was entertained to fuck. I really was. **1997**

My head's always been clogged up with fucking tunes and sounds and everything. I can't play an instrument though… I just can't. I don't think I'm capable. I mean I can fuck about. I can make something happen. It's just how I am. **1997**

Well, I won't be anywhere near as good as Dylan's writing in a million years. If people want to say that, that's cool, but I don't really think that. It's like if you are naturally a good driver or something. I can just naturally string words together. I've always done that. Even as a little kid I'd make up daft little rhymes about teacher to make the other kids laugh… it's nothing special. **1997**

It's only over the last couple of years that I've actually looked at myself as an artist, as a songwriter, as a musician. I would never admit to that before, you know. I didn't feel I was. Now I understand a bit more and I will say I'm a songwriter, or whatever. Now I'm actually hearing stuff from the Mondays coming out on compilations, or someone's playing it at a club or something, and I'm saying, that's pretty good for the year and that lot. **1997**

Oasis are good, man. For the last few years I've been tripped out on everything from Snoop to fucking Cypress to fucking Scarface. And Oasis are the first band to get me back to baggy-type music. **1997**

Oasis are doing exactly what they wanted to do, they same as we wanted to do. Liam had always wanted to be a rock 'n' roller, in a band, getting the chicks. At the end of the day, I think Noel and Liam are talented. No matter what shit they go through now and whether the band splits up or whatever. I think they are both genuinely strong enough, even though they are doing mad things now 'cos their heads are in loads of coke and they are saying lots of ridiculous things. That's all part of it, that's all part of them. Things will change for them.

It's like, imagine all your life since you was a little kid, you wanted this Jaguar and you get it and you are sitting in it and as soon as you turn the key it makes you sick. Something you've wanted all your life makes you sick with nerves. It's a shitty feeling and that's how it is for Noel and Liam, I presume. You'll need a big bag of coke to deal with half the shit they've got to deal with now. That was why I could never understand Kurt Cobain killing himself. All the dude had to do was take two years off, fuck his woman off, spend a bit of time with his kid, get himself strong. **1997**

I'm into Houston's Geto Boys at the moment. They are great, man, I love 'em. They've got it right. They've got the boom, man. You need the right tackle. You go back to the Sixties and dig out their tunes. Funky as fuck, guitars on 'em, what people are doin' now in the Nineties. Everyone of the Geto Boys, Bushwick, Willie D and Scarface, every one of them can write great lyrics. They basically do it like I do. Schoolboy made up fuckin' rhymes.

They're not glamourising violence, it's a comment on that sort of thing. You can listen to it and say, 'double heavy, right'? But, really, it's cartoon, man. I listen to this loads around the house. It makes you laugh, man. That's why I like it. Texas 'ip 'op. And it's naughty down there. They've just done another Geto Boys album and the fuckin'

boom on their bass is the loudest you'll ever hear. I've always been a funky head. I can't help me taste in music, can I? **1997**

Everyone goes on about all these people who combine dance and rock. But what about R & B, which is where rock and soul came from? That began as dance music. If the way I do things sounds natural, that's because it is natural. People have forgotten it, that's all. **1997**

I did say that I hated dance music once... I can explain that. You see, at that time I'd had just about enough of the whole fucking dance bollocks. I associated it with loads of shit that had happened to me, you know, drugs and stuff. And I just got to a certain point where I couldn't listen to the shit. Get in the middle of something and you get lost, man. Now I'm fine with that whole scene, but that's 'cos I'm not living it anymore. When you are heavily into a scene it gets very intense. For me it became too fucking intense. Now, like I say, I've got some distance on it. **1997**

At the time I really did fucking hate Suede. But I've got to admit now, since their last album, I've got a lot of respect for them and quite like a few of their tunes. There's lots of bands I slagged off in the Mondays. I mean, I really ruined the Inspiral Carpets' lives. But now, five or six years later, I listen back and a lot of their tunes are like what's happening in the

charts right now, and I think they are really good, y'know. That's one thing you learn. You waste a lot of energy slagging people for no particular reason. I respect anyone now who just gets up and has a go. That's why I now respect Suede and a lot of bands for having stayed at it.

When you first get well known in a band, and we were like this in the Mondays, you are all young and arrogant. Just because you have been on *Top Of The Pops* once, you think you are gonna be a megastar and you start acting like this motherfucking cunt. But then, after being in the business a few years you realise it's a privilege, a real honour to still be making records and it's great when people like it. **1997**

I'm not sitting here complaining about touring but I just wish I could do twenty gigs a year in really great places. Touring night after night all the time, that's why I tend to get so fucked up on the road all the time. Touring's just like a proper job, it really is, man. And the older you get the harder it gets. **1997**

Even in the Mondays I used to say, "Look dude, we haven't even done what Slade or Mud did. Kenny had more fucking top ten hits than we did." I measure my success by still being around in this business. But I'm not gonna be a lying cunt. I do like the dough and it's great that I can also make a couple of good albums and enjoy doing it. I'd be a fool to start moaning about it. **1997**

At the end of the day someone still gives us money to go in a studio and fuck about. And that's pretty cool. **1997**

Stinkin' Thinkin'...
Sex & Sexuality

Nah, we are not gay. We don't shag each other but we might hug each other every other now and then when we are pissed. When we are off our heads, it's love. Love, love all the way. **1992**

Lads who come from where I come from don't like being called a fucking faggot. I've got nothing against them, y'know what I mean? But I know my rights and I ain't a fuckin' faggot and that's it. You know what I mean. Fuck it I ain't going round bashin' 'em, I don't give a fuck. They can do what they want. But people, where I come from... rent boy... that's probably the worst thing you could call somebody. **1991**

I don't give a fuck it that offends people. I'm not really bothered. Before I came into this business, right, I came from the north of Manchester. I had never met a homo before... no, I hadn't. Ten years ago we was young boys and you come into this business and you meet gay people, right, and you think 'fuck'. But then you think, no. Sound. Leave them alone. So I haven't got any problems and I ain't a fucking rent boy and it was a dirty story on me. **1991**

None of our band are homophobic, right? Apart from him (Bez). If people read that interview I'm actually sticking up for homosexuals, but use the word 'fag'. I hate even going over it because it's like lying to put things right. But, in the first place, I've got nothing against homosexuals or anything... none of the band have. **1991**

I mean, people have tried it on with me. The man who did that interview – Steven Wells (*NME*) – he said that you can't blame it on the way you grew up. But teachers and the Catholic church and all that lot, they all say it is wrong. And when you've had fifteen years of schooling telling you that you have got to go out and live and go around places to find out that their attitude is wrong. **1992**

We got turned over in that interview. But that interview could have been written at any fucking point. That's how we always were, yeah, so we shot our mouths off. Most people do that but most people don't have some cunt standing in front of them with a microphone. We should have known. We were stupid and skagged up. I was off me fuckin' head and so was Bez. Bez has a heart of gold, everyone knows that. But what really, really pissed me off wasn't what was written at all, or the reaction of the twats who read and believe the *NME*, it was the rest of the band. The drummer, the bass player, the keyboardist. What a bunch of fucking hypocrites, man. **1992**

If you read the band interview in the *NME* about the homosexual thing, it was Bez who has his opinions on things like that. What got me into trouble was the choice of words... it offended people but I didn't mean it like that. **1992**

When you start defending yourself it's like, "Oh is he lying now to put the record straight?" To get sales back up, to get people coming back, and I'm not. And there are five people in this fuggin' band that have got no problems! Apologise! I'm not one for apologising. I never apologise, even when I'm in the wrong. But I'd like to apologise to all the people who got upset about it. **1993**

That's it... I've decided that I'm not going to make any jokes anymore. I've got to say straight afterwards, that was a joke. It's like Tony Wilson came out with this line about when Ian Curtis died, he made lots of money. And then there was all these letters in the papers saying how horrible he was. It's just the northern sense of humour. I know Tony loved Ian Curtis and if he could do anything to have Ian alive today, he'd have done it. **1992**

When I was on MTV, I said, I've changed me ways and I've got God and religion. If it hadn't been for Gaz laughing in the background that would have been a serious quote. It would have been the same thing as the rent boys situation again, I know that you can't have a sense of humour. You have got to be a serious twat all the time. **1992**

The gay thing did our heads in a bit, freaked us out for the fact that every-body who's ever met us in the business knows exactly how we are. Kirsty MacColl bollocked me about that gay thing, right, because she felt she had to defend herself to the people she knew saying "Look, Shaun ain't like that." I've read things in the papers people are supposed to have said and think, "You obnoxious twat. I hate you for saying that," but I know there's gay people out there who read that thing in the *NME* and know it's a load of bollocks. They know we are not anti-gay, or we hate this or we hate that.
   Even when we say things, it's just mouthing off like when you are talking to the lads. Showing off, I suppose, but Bez ain't capable of hating anyone. There's no excuse for what was said but people aren't just a pile of words. **1992**

Success has broadened my horizons, course it has. Like I just said, ten years ago I'd never met a fucking homo... when you make it you meet all sorts of weird people. Arteee people, go to arteee parties, things like that. Chill out, broaden your horizons on all sorts of things. **1992**

Gay? Me? No, I don't get turned on by dudes. But if I was gay, I'd fucking say so. **1997**

Casual sex? It's always depended on if I'm off me nut. With skag, some people don't want to shag but, fucking hell, sometimes I'd be going for like fifteen hours. You don't come, man, with skag. It takes a hell of a long time to come when you are on gear and it was great when the chick didn't know you were stoned. After an hour she'd be going, 'You haven't come yet, have you?' and I'd be thinking, fucking hell love, don't hold your breath, there's another fourteen hours to go yet. **1996**

Women think I'm a rough old crim. They think you're a bit nutty or something. But when we was growing up a lot of the women around, their old men were in prison, so, when you were 16 or 17 we got passed on to all these older ladies. So we got well fucking beaten into shape. That's why me ears stick out. **1996**

I've got nothing against women... fucking equal, that's it. When I did that *Penthouse* thing I did it 'cos I got paid. I don't care how they treat women. That's not my problem. You can put the argument that women read the maga-zines... women don't read the maga-zines... I don't give a fuck. I don't see women as dogs or anything like that. I just did it. I'm not bothered about why I did it or what other people say or what-ever. I don't care what people say about me. **1992**

Depends on what you call romance, mate. I call romance big boots and a big hot bed. I don't write songs for girls. You gotta be joking. Eucchhh! Caccky pooh pooh. Oh no, I've got a very bad ten-year old attitude towards girls. The closest thing to a love song I've written is 'Being A Friend'. And that's a straight out of Amsterdam porno song. Bit like a love song, I suppose. **1992**

I don't think I am irresistible to women. I mean, all me girlfriends have been alright. I was always this mischievous, naughty lad and a bit evil and ugly looking, and some chicks like that. In ten years I've had three serious relation-ships. In the first two relationships, I did fuck about a lot and I've stepped out of line once or twice with Oriole but because she grew up in the music business (her father is Donovan) she can deal with it better. She's seen a lot of shit and she's a strong woman. **1996**

I'm meant to be buying a house in Ireland in a few hours, We'd better get this inter-view done before she (Oriole, his girl-friend) comes and kills me. **1996**

Chicks turn me on. But I'm so into my woman it's unreal. It's probably the first time I've ever been in love. I'm not saying I've always been loyal to her but, in the past couple of years my head's been turned around. **1997**

Me and Oriole had this big argument. I broke the Hoover because she likes it and I feel bad about it. Very childish and very cruel. That Hoover! It bugs the shit out of me. It cost £700, the little fucker. **1997**

I'm banned from the local supermarket 'cos, if I go with Oriole, the bill comes to about £1000. I'm like, 'We gotta try those, we must try these.' I'm a real nightmare... so I'm banned. I'm only allowed to go to the local village shop where there's no choice. **1997**

I'm actually quite happy at the moment. I'm bang in love. I've got my kids, I'm happy, I really am. I really respect the girl, man. **1997**

I've never actually felt like that before. This is the first time. I'm not saying I haven't cheated on Oriole because I've been with her over five years, but respect has grown out of it. She is me top fucking friend and I can't cheat on her anymore. The blow out about me working too much, she understands, she grew up in the business. There's gonna be plenty of time when I can sit on me arse in a couple of years. **1997**

The kids come and get in bed with us, then they go and watch the telly, then Oriole will get up and we'll watch the telly have breakfast. Then we'll do something drive somewhere, go swimming. **1997**

The kids are into the fucking lot. They love the pictures, they love food, books, watching videos. I'm at the right time for all of that. Every other relationship I've been in I've fucked around, cheated about. I don't fuck about on Oriole. I don't want to. I treat her more like a mate. I've always been loyal to my

mates. If I did something behind me mates back I'd feel bad, but doping something behind me girlfriend's wouldn't worry me. But Oriole, she's actually me friend, me partner, everything. **1997**

Sometimes I get in the pool with the kids... though I'd rather sit around the pool with a brandy. The place where we go they'll serve you a brandy in or out of the pool. It's like a club sort of thing... in Ireland you can go down the pub and they don't mind kids being down there. When I'm not working I'm basically boring, I suppose. I like going for a pint, take the kids out, catch up on what's been going on the telly, watch videos and smoke weed. And shagging. I'm in me element really. **1997**

(On religion) I thought that was pretty cool, man, Clinton's been giving all the dough away. But when Clinton goes to Belfast – and I'm not giving my views on the IRA here – he's a hypocrite. He's shaking hands with the IRA and he's got a big smile on his kipper and he's acting as if they are Jesse James or Robin Hood. But if it was Castro going over there he'd be going mental. Why can't he do the same for Castro? Don't get me wrong, though, Ireland should be for the Irish and that's that. The Catholics should have what they want... but I'm not with Catholics or Protestants. I think everyone should live in peace.

It's ridiculous that we are still arguing over religion in this fucking century. Religion was the first rule book, the first common-sense book to keep the species alive. Like, if you live in the desert you don't eat pork 'cos it will kill your insides, get rid of your foreskin, make these fucking things up. "Thou shalt not do that, thou shalt not do this". Basically the Bible was the first fucking police force. Now we know a lot of this stuff, like Noah taking two animals here, two animals there, couldn't have fucking happened. But there's a message there and we know half of it is bollocks. It was just the first go at trying to be civilised. So why are we still arguing over this shit in the twentieth century? Everyone's just being tiny minded. These are traditions, let's treat them like traditions. **1995**

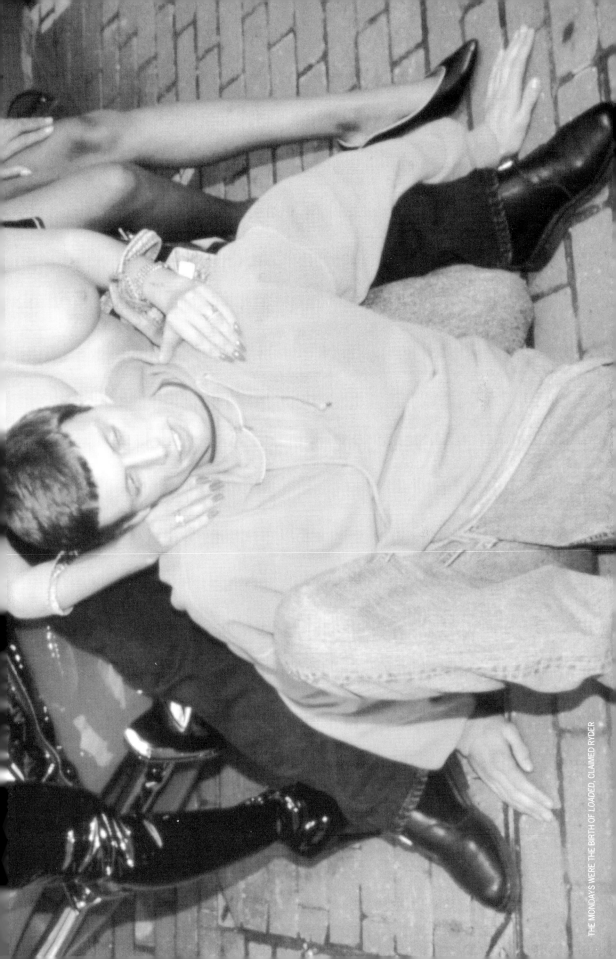

Ryder on Ryder

Well I've had a pony tail and I've had a portable phone and now I've got a skinhead and me phone's cut off...**1993**

It is a skinhead. I had me hair cut for the first time in ages and last night, I went into the pub to ask for some beers to take out and she's going, "It's £1.95 a can and I'm gonna ask if you can take that out..." I said, because of my fucking haircut, you cunt. I've got a thirteen hundred quid watch on...**1991**

I go up and down all the time... my weight goes up and down and everything. I might go on a drugs binge and I've got bags under me eyes and all sorts. And people think you're back on something when all it is one night of drinking too much and I look really bad. **1993**

I've nowt to hide. I don't fuck little girls. Anything else that I do, I don't give a fuck if they write about. I think morally and socially we're a double respectable band. All my priorities are well right and proper. **1991**

I'm lazy and hyperactive... both. It depends. If I've gotta do something, I'll do it. But when I've not got something to do, I just like doin' nothing. And then when I've not done anything for ages, I like doing something. What like? Staying in bed. Watching telly. Going out. Getting wrecked. Eating. Going places. All sorts. I like a nice day in bed some-times. Clubbing. I'm a night time person, always have been. It's the hours, innit? The hours go from about eleven o'clock at night to about eight in the morning then having a few hours kip until late, then get up. That's how it's always been, ain't it? Year after year. Just like nightshift workers. No need to do nine till five. Never done it, man, and I never will. **1997**

I still haven't grown up. I'm 29 and I still haven't grown up and I don't think a lot of men or boys do. Girls grow up when they are 15 or they've got their first nine babies or they're managing the house. Lads don't. They go out and do something that's like a fucking joke, innit? **1991**

I've always wanted to look good. My style's never really changed. I see pictures of me from '88 and I'm wearing shit people wear now. Nice leather jack-ets, anoraks, jeans, trainers. I'm still the same. Like I've got Patrick Cox shoes now but, even back then, I'd always try and get a decent make of shoe. I've always led the way in fashion a little bit. **1996**

Well we're always into that (Donovan). Especially when E came along, especially in Ibiza, at three in the morning when all the mellow tunes come on and it was double mellow E and all that. Donovan... mellow, mellow man, just sitting there, soaking it all in. Very Nineties. Very Sixties. Same fucking thing, man. Of course we are into Donovan. Why does that surprise people? When we first asked him to support us we thought all the older kids in the audience would like him and the younger ones wouldn't, but it turned out the other way. The young kids really enjoyed it and the older ones stood around stroking their chins and sayin "He's a fookin' old hippy", and thinkin' too hard about it. **1992**

I don't read a lot, y'know? I read bits of what I've said. If I've said it, then it's said. It's not much though. It's just in the paper innit? If I get slaughtered, it doesn't matter. I don't take it seriously. **1991**

Sometimes I like being dead nice and sometimes I like being a real cunt. I get a good buzz out of both. **1991**

I'm not shy... it's not like that, is it? If you don't really know someone and you are talkin' to them, you've not really got a lot

to talk about, 'ave you? Unless you hit something straight away or you are really pissed and you sit next to them and start talking about football for nine hours. **1997**

Look pal, if you are gonna start using big words like 'perceive' you'd better start explaining what they mean. **1992**

See my mind gets a bit noisy but I've been taking it a lot easier. You gotta. Meditation. Am I fuck! I'm not going out every night getting wrecked. We weren't any calmer making *Bummed*. In fact making it was the best four weeks of our lives. No fights. No troublemakers here. We can't stand being treated like shit, mind. You don't get treated like shit when you're at home. Then you go somewhere and you get treated like a piece of pooh. That gets us a bit mad. 'Cos it should be easy. **1992**

I got my dream at 18 years old. I got in a rock n' roll band. It's just the way my life has been. It's all been some sort of cartoon existence. Like the Bash Street Kids. The X-rated version. **1996**

It's all like a film. But I've been in a film since I was about twelve years old. Fuckin' hell. A bit unreal. Well cartoon. It's no particular cartoon, being in one though. I like cartoons. You gotta laugh at it. It's fuckin' hilarious innit? We take the piss out of everything. Don't matter what it is. When I say cartoon I mean everything going on around you can be real. You can have a real cartoon, can't ya? I'm making it up as I go along. Course I am. there's a lot of imagination in this group. **1997**

That's just the way the world is... and it's not as bad here as living in Russia, is it? You make your own opportunity. It's down to the individual. I ain't working at Tesco and another individual is and that's down to the individual's choice. **1991**

I'm standing there, in New York, with a bottle of Budweiser in my hand... and I'm just gonna put the bottle in his face 'cos I'm high on crack and I don't give a fuck about no gun. I was a bit startled though, when I thought about it afterwards and realised that nobody seemed particularly concerned. It ain't got that bad in Manchester yet. Well, it could be going that way. Makes you think... there I was, drawn into it, right into it and I'm like, pretty mild if the truth be told. If it can happen to me it can happen to anyone... not just the crack, It's the whole culture, the whole New York trip. Fucking screws you up, drags you in... you are part of the badness, the dark side and you don't fuckin' realise it. That was an eye opener, for sure. **1991**

People riot because they don't give a fuck and they want something for nothing. It's got nothing to do with fucking politics or nothing like that. Half the people who go rioting have got better trainers and better fucking stuff than people in middle class fucking housing estates... I don't give a fuck if that's a narrow view. I'm not sayin' I'm the world's greatest brain. I'm just me... **1992**

I don't get involved in any geographical expeditions. I don't read many books. I don't go on fuckin' protests. Fucking hell, I smoke dope, drink beer and listen to music. That's what I did. And the rest of it got built up. I got a house and some nice stuff... I mean it sounds negative but that's the mood I'm in now, know what I mean? **1996**

Shit, is this mine? Did I puke on myself? **1991**

I'm always feeling sorry for one thing or another. It just felt right, that's all. The band had done this mellow tune and it reminded me of one of Barney's New Order things. I'm not capable of writing a serious love song. I've always got to put something in to fuck things up a bit. **1992**

I've got me faults and I don't like 'em. I don't like 'em. **1994**

Tony Wilson compared us to Mozart! I can't be doing with all that bollocks. This is what happened to a lot of the members of the Mondays. For years they were surrounded by people telling them how wonderful they was. Some people in the music business act like they are fucking Al Capone, some big almighty force. They go around with this big attitude that they got it off the street and they earned big colours. To me it's just arty fucking dickheads who were all misfits who got together in a band and they are good or they are lucky or whatever. But this power that it carries really annoys me. I just thought Tony was a prick for saying that. **1997**

Class has got nothing to do with it, dude, what background a musician has got when it comes to making good music. When I was young I really had a fucking chip on my shoulder about shit like that but I certainly haven't now. I still feel I'm exactly the same. I am still working class. I can live in a bigger house but I basically feel the same. I'm a lot happier and more at ease with myself, but that's just through growing up. **1997**

You know, it surprises me that people ever expected anything more from us. We've got through all this just by being ourselves, which is a bunch of lying gibbering twats. Know what I mean? **1992**

It's always like that. Because we have found out that no one else quite lives in the same world as us. Those Spanish TV people were all right, but we can't go all smiley and be dead nice 'cos it just wouldn't be natural. So we live in our own little world and those media people have to just take what they can make of it... well, what do they make of it all? I've no idea. It's all mad, aint it? **1992**

The weather gets me up in the mornings. As soon as summer draws near, it's bet-ter, less numbing than the fall. That's when I get ambitious. **1997**

I love boxing. Fighting is a natural thing to man. **1997**

We (Shaun and Joe Strummer) talked about boxing. We were sayin' how other things other than drink or drugs can make yer trip. So in boxing right, you have the women coming round in their shorts at the start of each round. But you don't get some bird comin' on and whackin' herself off with a dildo, do yer? And that's because, if it's covered up, it's more effective for the state of mind of the boxer. Because in your head it releases this chemical, it gives you this ginseng rush to the body, sends you out there a bit perky, and right on it to go in smooth. But if there was a naked women in there giving herself a wank, you'd totally lose it. Know what I mean? And you wouldn't get the right chemical reaction. Yeah, we had a top intellectual conversation, me and Joe. **1997**

It's just me, me. That's me. All I'm sayin' is I'm just me. I'm not a poet or fuck all. I'm not sayin' these things to say I'm clever or logical. Half the things I say ain't logical but it's just what's in my head. **1992**

I can't really say I have any regrets because it has brought me to the person I am. **1997**

I do cry when I'm knackered. I get really angry with someone and fucking bawl them out, really give them a bollocking and then, afterwards, realise that I've been a dick and sort of trip out. **1997**

The last person I punched was a pal of mine, Gaz. He works for us. It was near the end of making the album and everyone was fucked and bad tempered. Me and Gaz had an argument, we'd been on some fucking cocaine binge. It was like a wrestling match, which is what happens when you are both drunk and off your head. **1997**

I'm not as selfish as my parents. I suppose I've got my old bloke's sense of humour and my mum's a bit sensible and

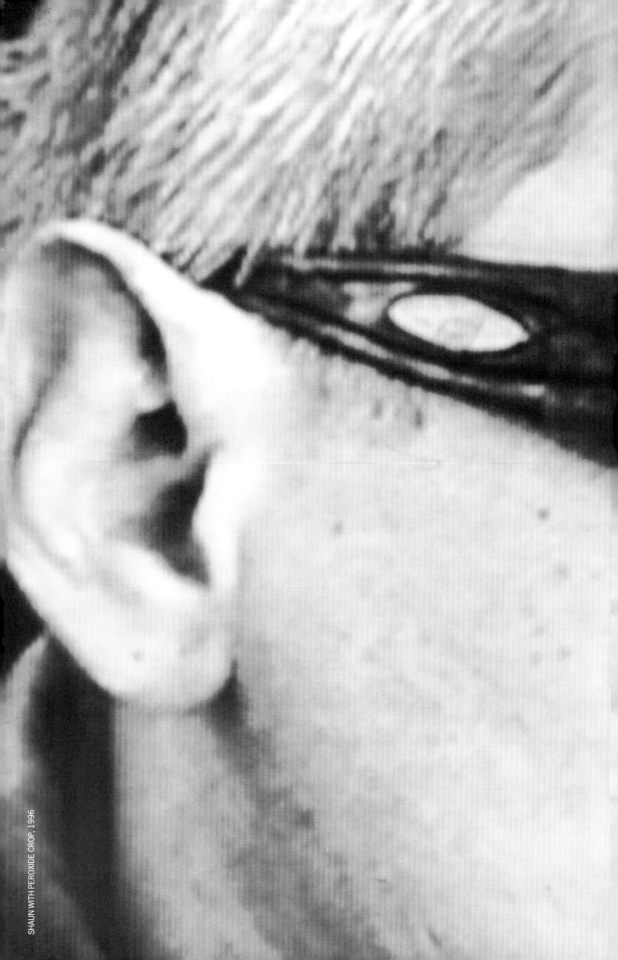

SHAUN WITH PEROXIDE CROP, 1996

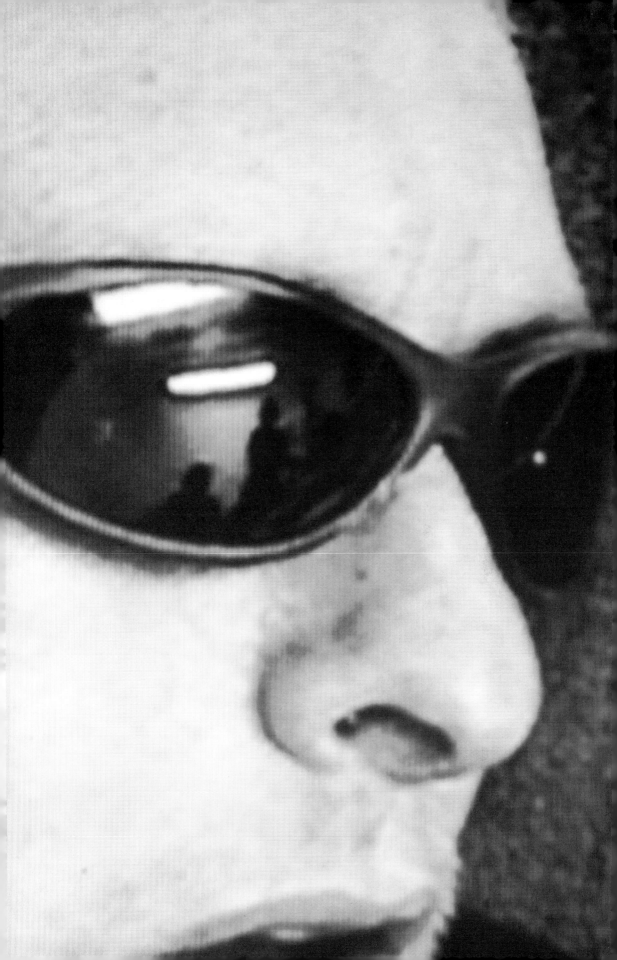

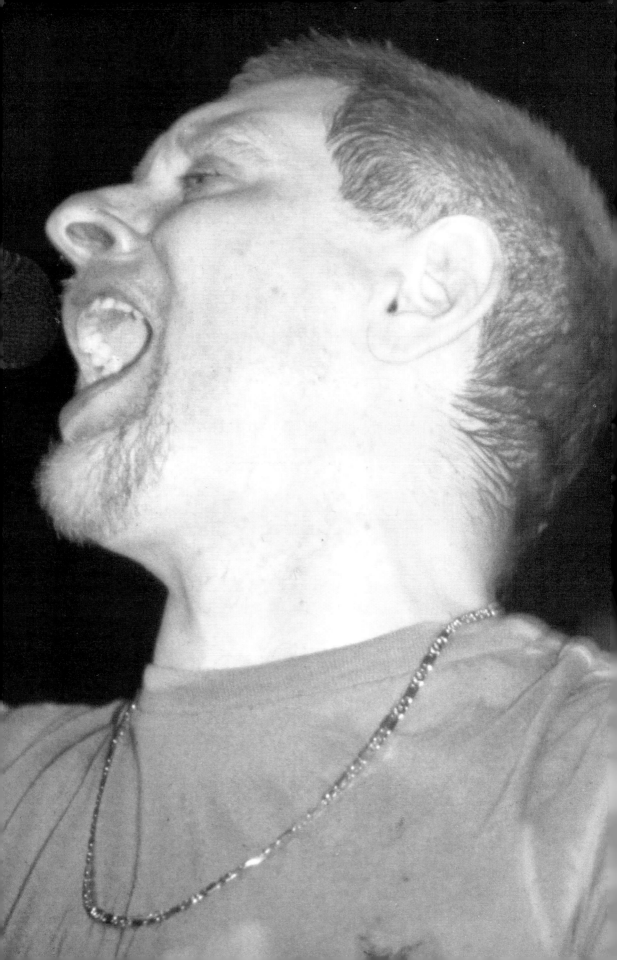

I am pretty sensible. I know when to pull back. I never get too far tripped out. **1997**

There has been progress though, despite all the negative things you might say about the Nineties. 'Cos when my mam was young they had an iron bath in the back yard and an outside khazi. And the poor was poor and the rich was rich... only richer. The old fucking monocled *Upstairs Downstairs* tackle. And if we go back to the 1880s, no cunt had a home. **1996**

I'd bring back capital punishment, but only if I could do it myself, and then only for child murderers... maybe. It's hard though because you know that in the brains of these people there is something missing, if you've got a speck too much or one speck too little you are way out of line. They should start checking out the balance in every cunt's head and take it from there. **1996**

My life has always been about the pursuit of making things nice... or pleasing meself or having a good time. It's pretty selfish really, but it's about entertaining oneself all the time. I'm on that buzz. **1997**

I can cook bacon and eggs, a stew, anything on toast. I can go to any nice restaurant I want but the trouble is my taste in food is just so fucking northern. The most exotic I get is lobster or monkfish. With chips. And it's got to have gravy. **1997**

You gotta order the fish, chips and mushy peas in here, they are wicked. **1997**

Before I gave up on education, when I was about 13, the one thing I did enjoy was writing stories. It was the only thing I ever got decent marks for. Alright, I would give them to the teacher and I'd actually be placed bottom of the class because I hadn't put the right full stops and commas in the right place, so my grammar was fucked. When that became apparent to me, that my story was better but other people were getting higher marks, I just totally gave up. **1997**

I wish I'd stuck with education... definitely. College I don't know about but my favourite TV programme in England is *The Learning Zone* on BBC 2, when everything else shuts down. But I just think when I was 13, 14, 15 I wasn't ready to be taught. **1997**

The telly has sent me mad in the past. I got into a bit of a depression when I was about 20. Kids' television drove me absolutely dolly... *Letterman*, Bravo Channel, TNT, Classic movies. A lot of talk shows get on me tits. The thing I'm always in trouble for is *Sky News*. I have it on for hours. I'd watch it around the clock. Oriole says it's the same every hour. I'm only allowed so many hours of news. **1997**

I'm not a boring cunt. I still like the odd night out. **1997**

When Diana died... I'd gone back to Manchester after a row with Oriole. I was with two of me pals and they put on the telly and all of a sudden they announced about Princess Diana... blah... blah... and all three of us, at the same time, went "Yesss! Woahhh! Yeasss!" And we all let out a big cheer and we were jumping. And it was like, why did we cheer and jump? There was about twenty million things going round in me head at once. I thought bollock-ings. I thought something wild. I wasn't cheering 'cos she'd been killed. It didn't hit me here. I felt really sorry for the kids, I thought William and Harry were very brave and they handled it very well, but a lot of it was unnecessary. I'm not a heartless twat but when people close to you die, then that really hurts, but I can't feel anything for someone I don't know. And I thought the music they put on, 'Sad bollocks in E fucking minor wank', I thought that was terrible. **1997**

Manchester's not a nice place to be at the moment. It's too small and everybody is fucking up. Seventy five percent of the people in this city carry guns. They all think they are gangster. There's so many fuckin idiots about the place now, it's unreal. **1993**

I live just a twenty-five minute plane ride away from me mam... So it's not like being on the other side of the world. I'm in Manchester all the time. I still love it but, no, I'm not going to plough everything I have back into the city. I've watched other people do that. I've watched them lose money. It's really hard work. They are all people who really care. Who are really passionate about what they do. I'm not like that. I just don't want to get involved in anything really, I want to keep it simple. Yeah... a simple life. Fucking hell, imagine me in local politics and all that shit. Never... never in a million fucking years would you get me sitting on loads of committees. **1997**

All I do in the film (*The Avengers*) is shoot Uzis, drive a Mini Cooper, have a knife fight with John Steed, shit like that. But I'm not really talking. Obviously, if I do get asked to do it again, which I have been, and if I like it, I will do it. But I don't see it as being a fucking great actor or anything. **1997**

I'm up early to do my last day's shooting on *The Avengers*, so it's got to be an early one tonight. I'll have a nice dump in the sink and then I'll retire to bed. **1997**

For my next film role I'm going to play the part of a little fucking big nose twat. **1997**

I'm certainly a lot happier now. Yeah. A lot more steady with myself. Obviously when we started the Mondays I was eighteen years old. All we ever were was daft kids who loved what they were doing. At the time I did like partying all the time, that's what a lot of young lads like doing. Now, when I'm touring or working like this, that is my play time. When I am not doing that I just stay at home with the family, chilling out. I like staying in, watching telly and smoking weed. That's it. I'm a boring sort of dude. **1997**

Mind you, they say life begins at 40. I might start going clubbing again. **1997**